T0064283

THE Fountain Pen PLUS FIVE

TATHAGATA MUKHOPADHYAY

THE
Fountain Pen
PLUS FIVE

PARTRIDGE

A Penguin Random House Company

To order additional copies of this book, contact
Partridge India
000 800 10062 62
orders.india@partridgepublishing.com

www.partridgepublishing.com/india
Tathagata Mukhopadhyay can be contacted at tmuprojects@gmail.com

Dedicated to the memory of Late Dr. Gurusankar Mukhopadhyay,
my Baba … my first teacher …

ACKNOWLEDGEMENTS

Call me Momma's boy if you want to – but without my Ma's blessings I would have been nowhere. Despite frail health and debilitative ailments, her positivity towards life helped me draw all courage and motivation for whatever little, professionally and personally, I did so far. Love you, Ma.

My wife and son comes next. They have always been with me in all my efforts, even when I lived alone, faraway, for many years of my life.

I am grateful to Sirshendu Mukhopadhyay, the numero-uno novelist of contemporary Bengal, twice recipient of Ananda Puraskar, recipient of Vidyasagar Award and Sahitya Academy Award for his literary works, for being the first critic of this book and writing its foreword. Sir, you have been my inspiration to write and would continue to be till I live.

I thank the leading fortnightly magazine from the Ananda Bazar Group, 'Sananda' and Ms. Aparna Sen, its erstwhile editor and Mr. Aniruddha Dhar, erstwhile assistant editor, for giving me the break as a writer, way back in 1993.

Then there are friends – hundreds of them – who helped me with their criticisms, and sometimes, thoughts and suggestions, which fueled my work. It's impossible to name them individually. However, there are a few names I wish to mention.

Rahul Guha – my schoolmate, now the Director, DGMS and photographer par excellence for the outstanding images used in the covers.

Malabika Mitra – my dear sis, for the wonderful illustrations to help the stories come alive.

Priyendrakishore Dutta – my friend who did the cold-eye-review and copyediting for this book, so if there are glaring mistakes, you know whom to catch.

Sandeep Mukherjee – for the extremely creative and artistic video promo for this book.

Parthasarati Chatterjee – my friend and ex-colleague – who kept egging me to resume writing, for after my fifth novel, I had stopped writing and gone into a long hiatus and kept finding reasons for doing so. Thanks Partha.

Finally, I thank all my readers in India and Bangladesh – all my previous works were in Bengali – and hope they continue to support me like they did before.

For now, enjoy "The Fountain Pen plus Five"…

FOREWORD

I first came to know about Tathagata when he stormed into the Bengali Literary circle, way back in 1991-92, when his first novel 'Pichchil' ('Slithery') was being serialized in 'Sananda'; one of the most popular magazines of West Bengal.

He had brought in a new dimension in Bengali Literature – that of hitherto unexplored domain of industrial whodunits, which had drawn a lot of attention from all quarters.

After this instant success, he penned four more novels in Bengali. While the backdrop of each of his novel was widely different from all the other ones, all his works had one common trait – that of pace and tempo. Once started – all his stories were virtually unputdownable.

This is one quality which he admirably maintained in his latest work – this time in English – a collection of long and short stories. Genres of the stories in "The Fountain Pen plus Five" are widely dissimilar, so are the styles. Tathagata has managed a seamless transformation from writing novels to short stories without compromising his USP – the ability to keep his readers captivated till the end with the bizarre twists and turns.

I am quite sure with this book Tathagata will easily multiply his reader-base, which hitherto was limited only to those who read Bengali; we will eagerly await his next work in English.

After going through the unique collection "The Fountain Pen plus Five", I have no doubts that Tathagata Mukhopadhyay, TM, is here to stay.

Sirshendu Mukhopadhyay
26 September 2015, Kolkata

"This is a work of fiction. Similarities with real life characters, if any, are purely coincidental."

CONTENTS

"Cogito, Ergo Sum …. I think, therefore I am"

Rene Descartes

THE HEIRESS

Aarey Milk Colony.

This is where I first met and got acquainted with Mr. Ahuja – popularly known as Ahuja Sahib or Ahuja Saab to everybody who went there for evening walks and jogs.

Aarey Milk Colony is a small wonder amidst the concrete jungle of Mumbai where rampant urbanization and unabated growth of buildings and traffic smothered the inhabitants day in and day out. Even today, it is refreshingly different from the sweaty Mumbai where people continuously jostled for breathing space.

It's an area covering several hundred acres which is used for milk and other dairy products. The Milk Colony was developed in collaboration with New Zealand which was complete with all aspects of dairy farming such as an educational institute, a research center, a calf breeding farm, staff and student quarters etc. You would find a 'New Zealand Hostel' amidst a hilltop inside the Aarey Milk Colony, which housed students pursuing studies and research on modern dairy technology.

It also was the home for rich tropical flora and fauna. Abundant rain in Mumbai ensures the place remains lush green year around. Even today Aarey boasted of a good number of leopards, its original natives, which can be sighted in deserted evenings. Why, even I had the good fortune of sighting them on two occasions!

Within five minutes, from sweaty-smoggy Mumbai, one could reach a place so green and rich in aroma of the wild! I doubt if there was any other place in the world where one could see such a radical geographic and topological transformation within five minutes of drive. One could immediately feel the cleansing effect in one's lungs after entering the woods of Aarey from the diesel-fumed Mumbai.

There were children's parks, a small pond for boating and a garden popularly termed as '*Chota* Kashmir' (mini-Kashmir) which were developed over the years by the Government of Maharashtra. But for me, and many like me, they were not the main attractions of Aarey. It provided us, the local Mumbaikars who stifle for space, with a fantastic opportunity for our daily calisthenics. We visited the hilly serpentine roads amidst the woods of Aarey for our regular morning and evening walks.

I categorized the visitors in Aarey into three distinct types. First – the walkers like me, who never believed in straining themselves too much. Walking was more of leisure than serious exercise. Second – the love-birds; couples, who sought intimate privacy from the hustle-bustle of Mumbai. Overly intimate lovey-dovey couples hidden behind bushes were not an uncommon sight. Third – the '*Joga-paglas*'; the serious joggers who huffed and puffed every day to keep fit. Joga is a name associated with *pagals* (mad men). For me, these fanatically obsessed joggers, who believed in persecuting themselves to keep fit through 'mad-jogging', were no less than *Joga-paglas*.

Ahuja Saab belonged to the first category, a leisurely walker, like me.

I took my evening walks on my way back from office. Luckily, I had to traverse the serene stretch of Aarey Milk Colony every day for my journey from my home to the office and back. It provided me with a great opportunity to park my Wagon R somewhere in between, slip on my sneakers and take a half-hour walk on my way back home every evening.

By virtue of being an everyday visitor, I slowly got acquainted with the other regular walkers. When you cross paths every day, you automatically develop a remote bond bred more out of cognitional motor skills than anything else. Bonds that start with the faintest of grins of recognition gradually extend to a slight nod of head or a wave of hand and then one day you stop to get introduced and have a few words…

Ahuja Saab walked with a slight limp, which generally happens to someone with difference in lengths in his right and left leg. And he walked very slowly. One could understand his sluggish gait for he was very old – middle eighties to be precise. The real reason for his perpetual limp, however, was not known. One more distinct characteristic of Ahuja Saab – one sniffed as one crossed him – unquestionably was the rich fragrance of expensive imported perfumes which he wore. A different one each day, the perfumes managed to overpower the natural aroma of the thickets.

I still recall the summer evening when we first got introduced. As I was walking uphill nearing the New Zealand Hostel, I saw Ahuja Saab crossing me with his seemingly labourious gait, when he signaled me to stop.

"Hello there, would you care to have a few words with this old man?" - He asked.

"Why; sure. Tell me Sir, what I can do for you."

That was the first time I saw him closely. He was a bald old man, short in stature but rather stout for his age, wearing a striped tee over a cotton trouser and a pair of sneakers.

"Nothing serious; I just thought we should get introduced. Hope I am not disturbing you young man?"

"No, no, not at all" – I replied, slightly embarrassed – "it's great of you to have taken this initiative. Who, these days, have the time to talk to bystanders, that too without any motive?"

"I like your style of walking. You have an air of confidence as you walk; very elegant. I had a friend who had the same style."

Now, who on earth does not like to hear a word of praise? Albeit a subtle embarrassment, I enjoyed his praise. Simultaneously, the cynic in me started questioning the real motive of this apparently harmless octogenarian. Why was this elderly gentleman trying to befriend me? As a matter of fact, I was very much aware that I had a very awkward style of walking – my wife told me this several times over. I heard Ahuja Saab continue his conversation,

"What's your age?" I told him my age.

"Hmmm … same as that of my middle son; well, I am Ahuja." – He offered his palm for a shake – "hope you are not getting disturbed or distracted?" I shook hands and said,

"Look Sir, why do you keep repeating this? Why should I be disturbed now?"

"Because, there are many who consider talking to a person like me a waste of time."

"No, no, please continue."

"Thanks" – Ahuja Saab was visibly pleased – "okay, take a guess on my age."

"Ummm … seventy five?" - I really tried my best guess.

"No son, I am ten years older – eighty five – yes, I am eighty five years young." - Ahuja Saab grinned mirthfully. I noticed that even his dentures were intact – unless, of course, they were artificial.

"I must say Ahuja Saab, I am impressed. You do not look a day older than seventy – perhaps seventy two. What's the secret of your youth?"

"Keep yourself happy. And take your regular walks. I have been coming here for the past twenty years. Everybody around knows me. Why, seeing me, even the BEST bus stops in the middle of two bus-stops, and asks me whether I would like to board – ha ha ha."

That was the beginning.

Thereafter, I started discovering Ahuja Saab gradually through our daily conversations. He had lost his wife about a decade back and lived alone in his apartment near Goregaon railway station. He had three sons – all married and settled abroad. His eldest son was a famous oncologist in New York. His second and third sons were settled in the Middle East. Ahuja Saab was very proud of his sons. However, he took more pride in declaring his self-sufficiency.

"I never take any financial help from my boys. I don't have to. I earn about thirty-thirty five grands a month through bank interests, which is more than adequate for me to sustain myself" - He often said.

"So why don't you wind up here and spend the rest of your life with your sons, daughters in law and grandchildren abroad? Living alone, at this age is not a good idea. Any day anything can happen. There may be a burglary, you may fall sick. With your kin around, you will be safe and happy."

"Me, living abroad – huh!" - He said with a hint of sneer – "I am in sound health you see, except for my eyes. Of late my eyes, especially the left one, are really troubling me. I quite enjoy my independence, my freedom. I don't want to be a burden on my sons and their families. Of course, I go once in a while for short trips, but never more than a month. I never like to be away from Mumbai for more than a month."

"Why so?"

"Mmmm … perhaps I miss this wonderful ambience, my morning and evening walks…"

Soon I discovered that Ahuja Saab was indeed a very popular man in Aarey Milk Colony. Sometimes I found him engrossed in deep conversations with a local milkman, sometimes walking alongside a young lass a quarter his age, sometimes walking the talk with middle aged housewife, Mrs. Bakshi and her big Labrador, yet another times with the Deputy Commissioner of Police, his vehicle and his personal bodyguards, softly purring behind…

I was never one of those mixing and socializing types. On my own I seldom introduced myself to somebody. But through Ahuja Saab, I got introduced to an array of regular walkers in Aarey Milk Colony. School teacher Shammi, TV serial actor Vinod Kapur, retired PSU Officer Ghai-Saab, housewife Pronita Bakshi, DCP Grover-Saab, bank-officer couple Kiran Gandhi and his wife – both choosing to exercise VRS and enjoy retired life, even Ashok Tambe, the security guard of New Zealand hostel, to name a few.

My curiosity regarding Ahuja Saab was ever increasing. Soon I realized that it was not me alone, everybody around were very curious about this octogenarian gentleman.

He most definitely valued his independence, otherwise why on earth would he be willing to stay all alone in Mumbai, when he had not one, not two but three well established sons? One required a lot of courage and conviction to live alone, independently. I came to know he got his daily meals from a nearby hotel, which in itself was a hardship for a person of his age.

"Why don't you migrate to America to your eldest son? I was told it was a land of plenty's. Life there is supposed to be the best."

"America? *Na Baba Na*. Dubai, Kuwait – still acceptable; at least, you can feel the whiff of India. But America? No way. I feel so out of sorts there."

Never did I come across any person who preferred Middle East to America. So my natural conclusion was, Ahuja Saab must not be in good terms with his eldest son or daughter in law.

Our gossips on Ahuja Saab increased with every passing day. After our walks, while cooling off in a group of four or five in the roadside wooden benches, discolored and semi-rotten with age,inevitably, we found Ahuja Saab coming up in our discussions.

Once,Ahuja Saab went missing for a week or so.

"Didn't see Ahuja Saab for a week; hope he's okay." – Said somebody from the group.

"For all you know, he must've left for Dubai – to his youngest son."

"No, no. I don't think so. He would have surely informed us before leaving. Besides, he hates to move out of Mumbai."

"Yes, he told me once. He likes Mumbai for this very place."

"That's nonsense. There are far cleaner and better parks for walks in America or Dubai. The fact is none of his sons are ready to accept him."

"But Ahuja Saab told me that all his sons are more than willing to house him. It's only his dogged aversion..."

"His sons may not be living abroad, for all you know."

"That's not quite true. Last time he got me chocolates from Dubai. Don't you get the fragrance of the imported perfumes he wears?"

"True. However, I have a feeling his sons may not be that well established as he claims to be. Living abroad does not necessarily mean one is well off. I know of many Indians who live abroad but live from hand to mouth."

"I still don't believe that his sons are settled abroad. These days, imported chocolates and perfumes are available in any of those modern malls."

"No, no. I'm not so sure about America, but I know for sure last year during the Dubai Shopping Festival, Ahuja Saab did visit Dubai. One of my neighbors happened to meet him at the Dubai duty free shop."

On that occasion, the real reason for Ahuja Saab's absence, as it turned out, was his aggravated eye-problems – particularly to the left one. Mrs. Bakshi, who was also missing all those days, took him to the eye specialist. That Mrs. Bakshi was also absent during all those days went completely unnoticed.

Ahuja Saab himself narrated the whole incident to a few of us after he'd gotten back.

"I never wanted to go to the specialist. The matter was not all that serious, you see. But Pronu won't leave me."

"Pronu?" - I was a trifle surprised.

"Pronu – Pronita Bakshi. She took all initiatives to seek an appointment with a specialist, and then took me to the hospital in her own car. Next day we again had to go for some further tests; and again on the next day. I tried my best to dissuade her, but she just won't listen. She didn't even allow me to pay for the petrol. Imagine, all the way from Goregaon to Dadar and back, four days at a stretch. Tell me these days which sane person goes so much out of the way to help anybody, that too for a useless old man like me? Even your own kids won't do this much."

Did I notice a hint of dissatisfaction in Ahuja Saab that day? Ignoring, I said,

"That's why, Ahuja Saab, I think you should go and stay with any of your sons;your sons, daughters in law, grandchildren – all part of you, your family."

"Are you not my own? Here I have friends like you, I have Pronu, DCP Saab, Ghai Saab, Shammi…"

"Well, I understand what Mrs. Bakshi did for you, but we, I mean the rest others, did nothing to help you. I think you should be a little more discreet in assessing and choosing your friends."

"Why, here you are talking to me, spending your precious time to hear the blabbers of an old useless person … you probably don't know but you are already giving me enough. One of the biggest enemies of old-age is solitude. As you grow old you will find that there are less and less people who would actually like to spend time with you…." - I couldn't hear the rest of the trailing mumbles of Ahuja Saab.

Little did Ahuja Saab realize that the kindness of Mrs. Pronita Bakshi of taking him to a specialist would fuel gossips in more ways than one.

A few days later again Ahuja Saab, and along with him Mrs. Pronita Bakshi, went missing. The walk-end gossips, this time, started with renewed vigour.

"Why has Mrs. Bakshi become all so protective and caring towards that stingy old man?"

"Stingy? Why stingy?"

"Then what; he, with all his wealth, can easily afford a chauffeur driven car. But look, he prefers to use BEST[1] bus instead."

"Ah, come on. His movements are mostly restricted from Goregaon station to Aarey Milk Colony, which is just fifteen minutes' ride in a direct bus. Also, all the staff in this route are known to him."

"No, no. Miser he is. Twice I dropped him at his place. Not once did he invite me to come in."

"May be he doesn't like your face. I too dropped him once. He invited me alright."

"But did he offer you anything?"

"What do you expect from an octogenarian widower; a feast? He did offer Danish chocolates after he returned from Dubai, didn't he?"

"Miser or not, I am sure he has a lot of riches; both in cash and kind. And that precisely is the reason why Mrs. Bakshi is so overly caring for Ahuja Saab."

If the bomb-of-a-gossip lay dormant for so long, its fuse had just been lit.

"Similar thoughts also crossed my mind, I must admit" – said a lady in the group.

"Rubbish. This is utter rubbish."

"What rubbish? Tell me why would anybody suddenly become so bloody empathetic for a person like Ahuja Saab so as to sacrifice her own time and take him to a specialist day after day after day in her own car, burning her own fuel? What's she got to gain?"

"I agree. It just can't be only on humanitarian grounds. Besides, there is something else I know which can only confirm this theory."

"And what's that?

---

[1] In Mumbai the State Transport Buses operate under the name of BEST – Brihanmumbai Electricity and State Transport – even though the electricity supply had long been disassociated with the State Transport department.

"Ahuja Saab himself confided in me once. His wife has left behind a lot of jewelries. Ever since he lost his wife, which is ten years from now, he doesn't know what to do with them. Now he's reached an age when, his good health notwithstanding, any day anything can happen. So he's getting very fidgety."

"This is complete nonsense. Ahuja Saab can easily divide the jewelries equally, or in whichever manner he liked, amongst his three daughters in law."

"Normally what you said sounds logical. But the problem is the old man doesn't want to give away his departed wife's jewelries and ornaments to his daughters in law."

"How do you know this?"

"He himself told me once. In all probability, he has told this to Mrs. Bakshi also. And ever since then, Mrs. Bakshi has become a mother-hen to Ahuja Saab. It's as simple as adding two plus two brother, you don't have to be a Sherlock Holmes."

What I gathered that day from the walk-end *adda* was not completely unfounded. I realized this after a few days when I met Ahuja Saab again. After exchanging pleasantries, Ahuja Saab asked me,

"I want your advice on some issue. Would you help me?"

"Advice from me? You are much more matured and experienced than I am, I really don't see how I can help you, but pray tell me. To the best of my ability I shall try."

"Ummm…actually I have some jewelry – my late wife's – you can say quite a good amount of various gold ornaments, some of them studded with twenty four carat diamonds. I really don't know what to do with them. In current valuation it would be about half a crore. What do you think I should do?"

Even though I half expected the advice Ahuja Saab was going to seek, I was nevertheless shocked. Was there really any ulterior motive behind the sudden fondness of Mrs. Bakshi towards this rich old man? Amidst the chirping of nest-bound birds, I heard Ahuja Saab say,

"I am really at a loss… there's a diamond set worth fifteen lakhs, then there are earrings, lockets, nose-rings, bangles – all made of pure twenty four carats. There is a diamond-studded nose-ring with a chain connected hair clip. Oh how gorgeous she looked when she wore this!"

In reminiscence of his late wife, I could see a rare glitter in Ahuja Saab's problematic eyes. Suddenly he appeared frail and helpless.

"Ahuja Saab – do you keep asking for the same advice to every person under the sun? I've heard about this from somebody else."

"No no, not everybody under the sun. I told this only to you and a few friends here, like you, whom I know I can trust. I may be partially blind, but I can see through my experience, ha ha... I know you are one amongst a few friends whom I can confide in."

"Still, Ahuja Saab, my first advice to you would be not to tell such things to all and sundry. You never know what's there in somebody's mind. Do you realize you are an extremely vulnerable target? Anybody can hire a local goon and kill you for money. You shouldn't be trumpeting around the stories of your late wife's assets."

"Ha ha... you are being a paranoid. So you think somebody will murder me for those jewelries? All his efforts would be wasted because the entire booty is in a bank-vault" – said Ahuja Saab twirling his thumb, as if he'd cracked the biggest joke of his life.

"You may laugh it off as a joke but..."

"Cut it, will you? Advise me on what I am asking for. What do I do with the jewelries?"

"It's you private matter Ahuja Saab. Since you are asking, I would advise you to distribute them amongst your daughters in law."

"No, no, never;that's not possible." - Suddenly Ahuja Saab became serious, paused for a while and then continued,

"My eldest *bahu* (Daughter-in-law) by virtue of living in America for so long now, is more American than an American native. Anything connected to Indian ethnicity doesn't appeal her at all. Indian art, culture, dress, jewelry, food – anything remotely Indian had little value to her. She won't understand the true value of the ornaments which has so much of family sentiments tagged with them. The heritage value of these ornaments would be lost if she were to lay her hands on it."

I did not quite understand what exactly Ahuja Saab meant by family sentiments and heritage value. It was more owing to *his own sentiments* which will be finished with his demise. However, I chose not to argue with him on that point and said,

"Fair enough; you can always sell the jewelries and divide the wealth amongst your sons. You may even choose to spend the money any which way you want, lead a more luxurious life. Maintain a good chauffer driven sedan, go on exotic holidays ... possibilities are endless."

"No, never. There are histories and anecdotes associated with each of these ornaments. So many memories, so many sentiments ... no no ... selling them is out of question. Never ask me to do that."

"Okay, then divide it between your second and third daughters in law" - I said, failing to suppress the hint of irritation in my voice for now I was getting a little tired of Ahuja Saab's unwavering stand against resolving the problem.

"My second daughter in law is not an Indian. She's a Palestinian. She can never understand the sentimental values associated with these jewelries."

Clearly, Ahuja Saab was not too pleased with his daughter in law number two. I was tempted to say that most women, irrespective of cast, creed and religion, always craved for jewelries and gold. However, considering Ahuja Saab's age and predicament, I chose not to open up that topic. I heard him say,

"My youngest daughter in law is the sweetest of them all. But the problem is she is very simple and much too driven by her ideologies. She never wears any makeup or ornaments. Several times I offered her to be the custodian of my wife's jewelries, only to be refused politely. She's not ready to use anything that has not been purchased from her husband's earnings; a fiercely independent lady – my youngest *bahu*. Wearing Ma-in-law's locket, for her is like wearing a chain of thorns! No, no, think of some other solution."

Needless to say, I couldn't advise much to Ahuja Saab on this account. It was evident that all my advice was given to him by others many times over, to which he turned deaf ears.

After I took leave from him I saw Pronita Bakshi arrive in her chauffer driven Maruti, the big benign-looking Labrador in tow, step down from her car and greet Ahuja Saab. For the first time I had a close look at Mrs. Bakshi. She was slightly built; the first signs of age-related weights cropping up in her rather attractive frame. Today she was wearing an evening gown instead of the regular churidar-kurti, her untied hair flailing in the free flowing breeze. She took Ahuja Saabs hands and together they slowly began to ascend the winding way before vanishing around a bend, all the while chit-chatting intimately...

Almost immediately, I started viewing Mrs. Pronita Bakshi and her motives from a different angle. Unquestionably, she was much closer to Ahuja Saab. If the octogenarian confided in me so much about his personal details, he must've disclosed much more to the middle aged housewife. May be he told her about his vault details. Who knew, he might have even shown the jewelries to Mrs. Bakshi. Senility can drive people to do crazy things and sight of gold and jewelry could drive people crazier, I was told.

My hunch became stronger after about a week, in course of yet another *adda* session in Aarey Milk Colony.

"Ghai Saab, you would drop dead if you'd seen what I saw last week… my my…"

"Hmmm … it looks as if you are dying to disclose some secret. Come on, out with it before you asphyxiate."

"Yeah, it appears you will have to make a trip to Hardwar to get rid of all sins you committed by your discovery."

"Indeed…indeed…I doubt if even a dip in the holy Ganges would be able to wash away all sins…"

"Come on tell us, allow us to share your sins…"

"Say what, I was on my scooter last afternoon, riding from Goregaon station to my place, when I saw Mrs. Bakshi emerging out of the flat complex where Ahuja Saab lives."

"Huh, only this? I thought you were going to break earth-shaking news? Must you dramatize everything? So many of us went to Ahuja Saab's place once in a while! Why, even you dropped him on your scooter once or twice, didn't you?"

"Yes, I could understand if the time was morning or evening, but how do you explain that at two in the afternoon?"

"Could be she had taken Ahuja Saab to a doctor, yet again."

"Do you think I am a fool to have not thought of that possibility? As soon as I spotted Pronita Bakshi, I stopped and tried to spot her car. She quietly hailed an auto-rickshaw and left. She was discreet enough not to use her car, since she doesn't herself drive. She never wanted any witness to her afternoon trysts, not even her driver – now do you understand?"

"Are you suggesting that this is the evolution of a modern 'Raas-Leela' – said somebody in the group with a lecherous grin, which I found rather distasteful."

"This is pure garbage" – I protested – "Mrs. Bakshi is like a daughter to Ahuja-Saab. You guys have this disgusting habit of whipping up gossips out of absolute non-events."

"Oh come on! We note your naivety, but think from the practical angle. Ahuja Saab has fifty lakhs worth of jewelries for disposal. That's a lot of wealth! Any woman, close to him, would be lured."

"Yes, fifty lakhs is worth at least fifty lays – if not more." - Surprisingly the risqué comment came from a lady in the group.

I left for home with a mixed feeling. There were occasions when Mrs. Bakshi and I happened to cross paths. She always smiled sweetly and exchanged polite pleasantries. Once in a while her husband accompanied her. She even introduced me to her husband. There was a temple inside the deep woods. She had offered me *prasad* from the Puja that she'd offered in that temple once while we met on our walks. It was very difficult for me to digest what I just heard about her from the group. It was challenging for me to picture Mrs. Pronita Bakshi as a scheming vamp, who was out there to exploit a rich old man with her feigned benevolence. To me she was a simple lady with a kind heart and deeply devoted to her family. She went out of the way to help Ahuja Saab only because her heart bled for the lonely old man and not with any devious intentions. However, the majority in my Aarey walker-group chose to believe otherwise. It was therefore difficult for me to ignore their theories altogether. It was a typical instance of ten people repeatedly claiming a deity to be a demon till the time one starts doubting one's own judgment as to whether the subject was indeed a deity or not!

Who knew, maybe all throughout I was wrong in my assessment. Difficult as it might seem, the group might actually be right in ascertaining the real motives of Mrs. Bakshi…

Thereafter amongst the group, even the smallest of incidents between Ahuja Saab and Mrs. Bakshi started making big news. For example, Ahuja Saab had this habit of touching the shoulder of his partner-in-walk once in a while. Now, his every touch on Mrs. Bakshi's shoulder implied a contorted connotation. People religiously started logging the exact amount of time Mrs. Bakshi spent with Ahuja Saab during their evening walks. That both of them arrived at the same time on most days for their walks was also not just a coincidence – postulated a few.

That, however, did not mean Ahuja-Saab had distanced himself from the rest of the group; far from it. He continued with his usual chit-chats with all others, me inclusive, like he always did. It's only through him I came to know one day that the problems of his left eye had aggravated. The ophthalmologist's medicines were clearly not working. He was finding it a little difficult to move around with eyesight in just one eye. His eldest son was arriving soon, and this time he was determined to take Ahuja Saab with him to New York for proper treatment…

And then, one day, Ahuja Saab stopped coming to Aarey Milk Colony for his daily walks. Coincidentally, Mrs. Pronita Bakshi also went missing. The pair became conspicuous by their absence! After about one – perhaps one and a half months – the gossips took a different turn.

"Didn't I tell you, something of this sort was going to happen? It was just a matter of time, wasn't it?"

"But didn't Ahuja Saab tell us he was leaving for America; to his elder son?"

"And also take his mistress in tow, right? How can you be so naïve? It's as transparent as water."

"I think Mrs. Bakshi's absence is sheer coincidence. See, where can an octogenarian gentleman like Mr. Ahuja leave except for his able sons? Don't stretch your imaginations to a point where you can stretch it no more."

"Don't be so sure brother. For all you know, he must've sold his properties here and settled somewhere else – even abroad – with his mistress. Don't forget, he had the money power! A rich old man, wasn't he?"

"C'mon, that's too much! Are you suggesting that Mrs Bakshi, just for the greed of Ahuja Saab's property, had ditched her settled marriage, family, car and even her pet Labrador and eloped with that old man whose days on earth are numbered? Write a soap named *'Karishma Kudrat Ka'* in Hindi for the TV channels. I'm sure;some soap producer would lap it up!"

"Whatever you may opine brother, I have a feeling that this is no coincidence…"

***

The advent of monsoon in Mumbai was dramatic. It arrived almost inevitably at a pre-appointed date, season after season, almost as if the weather-God also wanted to contribute His bit to the professionalism of Mumbai. You would wake up one morning, usually between the first and second week of June, with a heavily overcast sky, which soon breaks into heavy incessant precipitation – that would continue for a week! Suddenly all the grime and heat and dust of big bad Mumbai would be wiped off, and the flora of Aarey would get a healthy green hue in matter of days…Number of joggers, strollers and lovers reduced drastically in the monsoon soaked Aarey. Croaking of lovelorn toads and chirps of crickets added to the eeriness amidst the shrubs and bushes, which all on a sudden assumed a healthy glow. The winding streets through the hillock of New Zealand hostel got almost deserted, save for a few like me, who enjoyed their rain drenched walks.

One such rainy evening, as I was completing my walk, I saw few labourers unloading concrete benches from a lorry by the side of the road. A woman, face hidden behind her unfurled umbrella,was supervising the process. Then I noticed the familiar white Maruti and the big white Labrador peeking out of the rear window of the car…

Mrs. Pronita Bakshi … !

Almost with subconscious spontaneity, I sauntered across to where Pronita Bakshi was standing, a rush of memories and gossips inundating my mind. In an instant she spotted me, and offered her familiar smile of recognition.

"Hey Mrs. Bakshi, what are you doing here in this rainy deserted evening? It can be dangerous. Do you know there are leopards around?"

She chuckled, and replied,

"In that case you are equally at danger. Besides, I have Bagha to take care of me" – she pointed towards the rather benign looking Labrador, happy to keep himself dry and cozy inside the car. I was sure Bagha would never step out in the rain to save his mistress in distress, should the occasion arise.

"Don't get wet in the rain, come; come, under this umbrella" – she beckoned me under her open umbrella.

"I am already drenched" – I said, but took a few steps forward towards the lady, nevertheless. Close enough to get a whiff of the imported perfume she was wearing!

"So what's happening?" I asked.

"What to do; I got delivery of these concrete benches today. Where am I going to lug them around? It's best to place them at their locations. Will have to fix them to the ground later; can't leave them loose like this forever or else these will be stolen."

I slowly walked alongside her towards a bench placed under a lamppost with a high-powered sodium vapour lamp glowing brightly, dissipating the darkness that was slowly but steadily engulfing the surroundings.

It was a solidly constructed concrete bench coated with red mosaic. On the back rest there was an engraving which read *"My small initiative for the weary travelers who wish to rest their limbs a while – Vinit Ahuja".*

Oh, so Vinit was Mr Ahuja's name. Strange, it never had occurred to me that Ahuja Saab, like all of us, also had a first name. To me he was only Ahuja Saab!

Nevertheless, I couldn't help asking,

"Vinit Ahuja – is that our Ahuja Saab?

"Oh, you didn't know? Of course, how would you have known, he hardly ever disclosed his first name to anybody."

"Where is our good old man now?"

I asked with a little trepidation, fearing the worst. By then, I was more or less sure that I would get all of Ahuja Saab's whereabouts from Mrs. Bakshi, irrespective of whatever relationships they shared.

The unloading was almost done, save for one. Mrs. Bakshi instructed the lorry driver to proceed to the next lamp-post which was about two hundred meters away for unloading, and then said,

"Come let's walk – you can come under the umbrella, it's still drizzling."

As I walked alongside Mrs. Bakshi, I enquired once more,

"But Ahuja Saab …what about –"

"He's no more" - said Mrs. Bakshi, almost inaudibly.

"What!"

For some reason the news hit me hard even though I was expecting it. Anything could happen any day to an eighty five year old man, yet that evening it somehow left a lasting impact on me. Or perhaps it was the eerie surrounding that was responsible…

"Yes, it's almost a month now; in Chennai."

From her voice I could make out that Mrs. Bakshi was on the verge of breaking down.

"But he was having sound health? How, all on a sudden…"

"He almost went blind in his left eye. We decided to consult Shankar Netralaya in Chennai. Ahh…it was my decision, really. The doctors there operated on his eye, and then somehow he contracted an infection … no antibiotics worked … complications went on multiplying … he was moved to the Apollo Hospital. His conditions deteriorated rapidly. His vital organs, one after another, stopped functioning. And then one day his heart stopped."

Mrs. Bakshi was now sobbing uncontrollably. I had no doubts that Ahuja Saab's demise had impacted her hugely. She, I could see, was holding herself responsible for this tragedy. My hunch was confirmed when I heard her say.

"I shouldn't have forced him to go to Chennai. He was managing well with his right eye. He could have easily lived a few more years. I… only I am responsible for this…"

"I don't think it's proper for you to blame yourself. Whatever decision you took was for his well-being, wasn't it? How were you to know that a minor operation could lead to such severe infection? As far as I know, his sons live abroad. Weren't they present during his last days?"

"His elder son flew in from America, his middle son from Dubai. But none of them could be present to perform the last rites. By the time they arrived, it was all over. Everything happened so swiftly…." - mumbled Mrs. Bakshi.

"What about his youngest son and his wife. Ahuja Saab was particularly fond of his youngest *bahu* – he had confided in me once."

Mrs. Bakshi somewhat managed to gain control over her emotions. Wiping tears with her handkerchief, she said,

"He never kept any relations with his youngest son. To him he was as good as dead. They never communicated with each other for years…"

While this news of Mr Ahuja's broken relationship with his youngest son came as a minor shock to me, the old thorn of suspicion started pricking me yet again… How on earth did Mrs. Bakshi manage to know so much about Ahuja Saab and his family? That she was very close to him was no secret, but *how close* was *very close*? Should I ask her point blank on her relationship with Mr Ahuja? Wouldn't it be too gross? As I was weighing the pros and cons of whether or not to ask Pronita Bakshi my inquisitions I saw her wipe her fair nose till it turned pale crimson and say,

"It's good we met here today. Before his death Ahuja Saab remembered you."

"Me?" - My astonishment knew no bounds! – "But he hardly knew me!" - I exclaimed.

"Yes. You; he had this extraordinary skill of gauging people even through the limited exchanges he had had with them."

"And what was his opinion on me?"

"He held you in very high esteem. He told me to consult you should I face any problems in future."

"Consult me; what for?"

"On anything, any earthly matters;he told me for whatever you were, you would never cheat anybody. Today I want a few advice from you. Would you oblige Mr. Mukhopadhyay?"

By now I could feel an extra tautness in all my senses. What exactly was Mrs. Bakshi planning to ask of me? I only hoped it had got nothing to do with Ahuja Saab's jewelries and ornaments.

"Ok, ask" – my voice cracked a little as I replied.

"Ummm…I don't know how to make a start. Well, as the testator, he had given me all his properties through a will. I am now the legal heiress of his flat, his bank deposits and also the jewelries that belonged to his late wife. Honestly, I do not need any of his riches. I therefore used up bulk of his bank deposits, cash and share certificates for these benevolent causes, like installing these benches, planting trees all over Mumbai and so forth. I also plan to sell his flat and open a trust for orphans and special children to cater for their studies. The problem is with the jewelries. I have no clues as to what to do with them. You see, I do not wear any jewelry. But they have so much sentimental value attached that selling them would be a breach of trust for his departed soul. He trusted me so much. Before his death, he pleaded me not to sell them…in fact he wanted me to use them…"

I saw Mrs. Bakshi on the verge of breaking down, yet again.

I cleared my voice, and asked her point blank,

"Pray tell me Mrs. Bakshi, did you have any relationship with Ahuja Saab? Before I advise you anything on this, it's important I know the truth."

She did not immediately answer.

I, however, was persistent.

"You have to tell me dear Lady, what made you so close to Ahuja Saab? Why on earth did you go out of the way to take care of his well-being, and why the hell did he write every last bit of his nickel on your name when he had legal heirs in his three sons?"

Mrs. Bakshi chuckled, mirthlessly. She weighed her thoughts in her mind for a while before letting them go,

"Why, didn't you hear any stories on our so called relationships?"

"Stories? What stories?" - I feigned innocence but it sounded unconvincing even to my own ears.

"C'mon mister; luscious rumors involving Ahuja Saab and me completed full circles and managed to reach even my ears, and you are telling me you haven't heard anything at all? How am I to believe that?"

"Oh that. I overheard something; some gossips, but did not believe a word. Usually, I distance myself from such gossips. Not my style. Now, hopefully, you will come out with the truth."

"Come; let's inaugurate that newly laid bench, shall we?" - She beckoned me to sit beside her.

I sat beside her in the semi darkness. Save for the croaking toads, screeching crickets and pitter-patter of the steady drizzle, everything was spookily silent. The sodium vapor lamps were fighting a losing battle against the pitch darkness of the Aarey woods. In the semi darkness, Mrs Bakshi's profile loomed like a fairy-tale princess. Fragrance emanating from her body, now stronger because I was downwind, almost brought Ahuja Saab back to life.

Mrs. Bakshi took a deep breath, regained some poise and started:

"Many years back, Ahuja Saab was posted in Calcutta. He, along with his wife and youngest son Vipul, lived in a rented house in New Alipore; our house. They lived in the ground floor while I with my parents lived in the first floor of our two storied home. I was very small, small enough to move around in Ahuja Uncle's laps. His elder two sons lived in residential hostels, and would only come home during holidays. Right from those days Uncle was very fond of me. He always aspired for a daughter. May be in me she found the daughter which he never could have. When I was in eighth or ninth standard, Ahuja Uncle got transferred to Bombay. Those days Mumbai was still Bombay and Kolkata was Calcutta. This however, was not a deterrent to break all contacts with us. He wrote to me regularly, telephoned me occasionally and even parceled me new dresses for the Pujas. By virtue of living so long in Calcutta, Uncle was aware of all Bengali festivals and rituals. Five, perhaps six years passed. I got into a college. One fine morning Ahuja Uncle arrived in Calcutta, unannounced, with a marriage proposal. He wanted me as the bride for his youngest son Vipul. My parents, initially, were a little circumspect. How could a Bengali middle class girl, brought up in a Bengali culture adjust in a Punjabi family that was culturally so different? However, Ahuja Uncle was not ready to relent so easily. Ultimately, his dogged persistence paid off. From my side I had no problems. Vipul was four years older to me, and I knew him well enough to have my fears allayed, even though we were not in any relationship.

So I had agreed. And then, ten years back, we got married, I must say, rather ceremoniously…"

I was completely flabbergasted! I simply couldn't believe my ears.

Mrs. Bakshi is Ahuja Saab's youngest *bahu*! How on earth was that possible? She a Bakshi, her husband an Ahuja…

Pronita Bakshi was sharp enough to read my mind. She continued with her amazing life story…

"Life is not always fulfilling, Mr. Mukhopadhyay. Sometimes it can be cruel too. Soon after our marriage, we discovered Vipul and I had compatibility problems. I would not go into details why, because it's not important in today's context. All I can say is the proposal of divorce came from Vipul. Ahuja Saab – my papa-in-law – tried his best to persuade Vipul, but all his efforts were of no avail. Finally, in a blind fit of rage, he ordered him out of his home. Vipul, with all the adamancy he'd inherited, left his home forever. My papa-in-law stood by me. 'Don't worry Pronu. As long as I am alive, no evil can ever touch you. I dented your life and I will make it up for you. I will get you married again – just keep faith in me girl' – he had said."

Mrs. Bakshi started sobbing again, uncontrollably, like a child.

"And soon enough' – she she said, weeping, – 'he found a suitable Punjabi match for me. Mr. Bakshi, my second husband, accepted me unconditionally…"

"In that event, Mrs. Bakshi, I suggest you do nothing with the jewelries, just keep them in the bank vault. Give it to your daughter or daughter-in-law who would proudly carry the Ahuja-Saab's family tradition and sentiments to the generation next…and then the generation after…"

The rain intensified, and with it Mrs. Bakshi's wailings…

***

I left the place with a pall of gloom and shame. The reason for gloom was largely because of Ahuja Saab's demise. He, indeed, was a kind hearted and jovial soul. I felt shameful, for I stooped so low in assessing a clean and simple person like Pronita Bakshi. Shameful for being so judgmental, for allowing my intellect to clog and get influenced by petty gossips…

Soon after this, I came to learn that Mrs Pronita Bakshi had moved out of Mumbai with her family. I do not know where, nor was I interested in knowing, because for me it was a closed chapter. Only the sturdy concrete benches remained there as a legacy of a young-old man – Vinit Ahuja…

My story could have easily ended here, but for an incident that happened about a year after Mrs. Bakshi left Mumbai for good. It was just the beginning of winter – if one could classify that as winter – in Mumbai. It was well past Diwali, and the plumage in Aarey started losing it lushness with the advent of the fall. Memories of Ahuja Saab had faded considerably from our minds – the concrete benches notwithstanding. I spotted the huge black Mercedes just behind my puny little Wagon R, by the roadside on our usual walking track.

I – for that matter anybody – couldn't have missed it. Even though Mercedes is not so much of a rarity in Mumbai, there was nobody in the group who had this treasured possession. The car came again on the next day, and again the day after. It wasn't very difficult to identify the owners of the spanking new machine. A good looking, made-for-each-other type middle aged couple, dressed nattily in branded tracks and sneakers, along with head bands and other jogging accessories. We got two new inclusions in our group of walkers. As usual, daily meeting bred familiarity, which slowly transcended into smiles, friendly wave of hands and finally a formal introduction by shaking hands. With the new couple also it wasn't different. Very soon they got introduced to the whole group little by little.

One evening as I was parking my car behind his, the couple came down, locked his car with a flick of his remote and the man proffered his hand to me,

"Hi, I am Ahuja. Vipul Ahuja. Meet my wife, Sunita Ahuja."

I introduced myself and asked,

"New in Mumbai?"

"Ummm – ya, in a way yes. Returning to home town after long, long, time is almost akin to arriving at a new city. Besides, Mumbai has undergone a sea change in its infrastructures."

"Are you suggesting Mumbai was your home town?"

"Most definitely;this was where I completed my student life and started my professional career."

"By the way, your name made me curious. Do you happen to be in relation with one Mr Vinit Ahuja? He was a regular visitor to this place."

"Oh yes. You guessed it right. He was my Papa. In fact my first visit to Aarey was with my Papa. I was still in school. This place used to be lonelier. Now I see a lot of vehicular traffic."

"I knew your Papa. He was a very nice and kind hearted person. But you were settled in the Middle East, weren't you?"

"Yeah - but how do you know, oh I see, Papa must've told you, right?"

"Yes, he often told stories about his sons and daughters-in-laws. So what brought you back to India?"

"I got a good offer in Mumbai. Honestly, there's no place like home. I am glad I came back after spending fifteen long years in the Middle East, even though Sunita here doesn't sometimes agree" - said Vipul with a mischievous wink – "she got too used to the Arabic lifestyle!"

I looked at Vipul's pretty wife. She was a coy lady with wide deep-set eyes and springy curls leashed by an Adidas head-band who – unlike an average Indian middle aged woman – had maintained herself well with controlled diet and calisthenics. He must have married him after his first marriage with Pronita failed; the natural thought that crossed my mind. "So where did you get to meet each other, Madam?" – I asked, more to continue with the conversation than anything else.

"Why, here, in Mumbai. I am very much a Bombayite, like him" – she said.

"Yes, we got married just before I left for Dubai, didn't we Sunita? That was about fifteen years ago. How time flies!"

Fifteen years! Vipul's disclosure started reverberating in my ears with ever increasing intensity. Didn't Mrs. Bakshi tell me a year back on the eventful monsoon dusk, here at this very location, that she got married to Ahuja Saab's youngest son, Vipul about ten years ago, which is about eleven years ago from now...?

Vipul and his wife were carrying on some conversations on this and that on Mumbai, its past, present etcetera; only I wasn't listening any more. I was in no state to listen, for my mind was occupied with all the events on that fateful rain-soaked evening in Aarey with the fair and innocent heiress of Ahuja Saab that kept re-playing over and over again kaleidoscopically...

PANDIT

Rupali and Kairi.

No, they are not the names of beautiful damsels. They are the twin movie halls in the sleepy town of Chinsurah that has managed to last through the sands of time, and together is still very much a huge landmark and the chief entertainment hub of the town.

In this age movies are synonymous with multiplexes. Stand-alone halls are inevitably gobbled up by either multiplexes or shopping malls. Therefore, the sustainability of the two grand old ladies, Rupali and Kairi, is indeed a small wonder.

Rupali and Kairi were a part of my daily life as I grew up in Chinsurah.

The two movie halls were separated by a wall. One could easily cross the wall - it also had a gaping hole - and move to-and-fro between the two talkies. In a sense, this too was an early concept of a twin-screen multiplex. And within the compounds of the two halls, like modern multiplexes, there were eateries, sweet-shops, chemists and the omnipresent *paan*-cigarette stalls.

This is the place where I slowly got inducted into the so called 'bad' world.

This is where I first bunked school and saw an Uttam-Suchitra matinee.

This is where I had my first drag off a cigarette.

This is where I saw many a relationship culminate and terminate; mine inclusive.

This is where I had my first place of *adda,* and this is where I befriended a huge bandwidth of friends ranging from scholars, who managed to secure State ranks in School Leaving Exams, to garage mechanics, to hall-ushers and even those who sold movie tickets with a premium — commonly known as ticket-*blackers* or black-*marketeers* — for a living.

The Police Station (for some reason it was known as the Police-Line in Chinsurah) was just across the road on which these twin halls were located. We were even pally with Jagadish-da, Utpal-da, Poran-da and a few others who were cops in that Police Station. On packed shows, they often had surveillance duties at the hall premises to manage the law-and-order. Despite that, black-marketing went on unabated setting a unique example of peaceful coexistence of the hunter and the prey!

Those days, after radios, movies (also colloquially referred as 'pictures') were the chief source of entertainment. We waited eagerly for a new Hindi or Bengali release. Dev Anand, Dilip Kumar, Saira Banu, Vyjayantimala, Uttam Kumar, Soumitra Chatterjee, Supriya Chowdhury, Dharmendra, Suchitra

Sen – were big stars. Their movies inevitably opened with packed halls. There was no advance booking in either Rupali or Kairi. So there were long queues for tickets. Queue for two PM matinee show started as early as ten, sometimes nine AM. Crowds thinned out within a week if the movie was a flop, but inevitably, the first-day-first-show used to be a sell-out.

First-day-first-show used to be a craze! First-hand review of a movie provided one of an opportunity for one-upmanship in one's friend-circle. And that was a field-day for my black-*marketeer* friends! A 45 paisa ticket could fetch a price as high as rupees 10 and a 'First Class' ticket, costing 2.10 rupees could even fetch rupees 40-50. Rupees 50, in those days, was a big amount, considering the facts that my school tuition fees was only rupees 5.50 per month, a cup of tea at Sen-Cabin cost 10 paisa, a packet of ten Charminar – 30 paisa, and one could get four yummy *sandeshes* (sweetmeats made of fresh cottage cheese) from Sandhyashree Sweets for a rupee!

Pandit was the star black-*marketeer* in the complex.

He was a wiry person with thinning hairline and surprisingly calm and sleepy eyes. His lips were perpetually red for his habit of continuous *paan*-chewing. He hailed from Bihar or Uttar Pradesh, but spoke passable Bengali. But his skills in maintaining good public relations were outstanding. He always had a friendly curl-of-a-smile, and befriended everybody with equal ease. He was friends even with the local cops, so much so that he continued his business of selling tickets at a premium right under the noses of the cops.

Pandit was a friend. I do not remember when or how our friendship developed, but we became thick of friends. Having Pandit as a friend had its benefits. For example, after befriending Pandit, I never had to bother for a first-day-first-show entry. He gave me ticket at a very low premium – but never at actuals. After all it was his *dhanda* (business). It's not just entry, Pandit could manage seats of one's choice.

Sen-Cabin - a small eatery in Rupali's compound, which served delicious devil-chops and tea, was a popular tryst for couples. Sen-Cabin had a partitioned row of four-five 'cabins' – which provided 'privacy' behind translucent plastic curtains. They were meant for 'family' – but were mostly used by truant school and college going couples. In those days, dating was limited to viewing matinee shows and then snacking in joints like Sen-Cabin, before calling it a day before dusk. Urmi and I were occasional visitors, but more about that later.

Pandit arranged for premium seats for young couples, of course at an extra price!

Bilu-da was a multi-tasking employee of Rupali. He was tall, well built with an angular and very serious face. He rarely smiled. He always wore a full-sleeved shirt, un-tucked, with the sleeves rolled up to display his sinewy biceps. I saw him selling tickets at the booking counter, ushering patrons and helping them to find their seats with his torch-beam and also, usually in the mornings (the first show was always at 2 pm) patrolling the streets of Chinsurah on a cycle rickshaw distributing hand-bills for the current movie as well as the forthcoming releases – all the while shouting through a battery operated microphone and publicizing the movie with its star-cast and other attractions. He managed to modulate his voice dramatically, so much so, even the ladies, young and old, peeked through their windows and verandahs, to hear his announcements. In between announcements, he would play soundtracks of the very movie. Bilu-da mastered this art of presenting superb audio-trailers of the movies. His announcements went something like:

Music...music...music...
(Music fades out and Bilu-da's voice blurts out)
Come one...come all...releasing next Fridaaaaaaay....
Super star Utttttam Kumaaar and his favorite romantic heroine.......
Yeah...yeah...yeah...you guessed it right....Mahanaikaa Supriyaaaaa.....
In the best musical hit of the yeaaar.....
CHIRADINER......
Next Friday, 23rd August......Rupaaaaaliiiiiii
(Music...music...mucsic....)
Every day three shows... two, five and eight pm....
You cannot afford to miss....You won't want to miss... Mahanayak Uttamkumaaaar romancing Mahanaika Supriyaaaaa......in the biggest musical extravaganza of the decade.....
CHIRODINER....Rupaaaaliiii...Next Friday....23rd August.....
(Music...music...music...)
Haunting music by Nachiketaaaa Ghooooose....which will not allow to sleeeeep.....
CHIRODINER...
(Music music music)

Bilu-da would single handedly announce, control the volume of the music played on a record player on his lap wired to his microphone and also stick the hand-bills on the proffered palms of bystanders and the urchins running behind his cycle rickshaw. Amazing talent!

Sometimes the proprietor of Kairi Talkies would also hire Bilu-da's service for publicity.

Rupali and Kairi had different proprietors, so in a way they were competitors. But strangely, there were no animosity between the two. In fact they made it a point to release movies of different genres, so that they cover the same mass twice over. If Rupali came up with a Uttam-Suchitra starrer Bengali family drama, Kairi aimed for a Dharmendra-Waheeda starrer Hindi action flick. Entertainment starved Hooghly-Chinsurah public lapped up both!

Pandit, using his extraordinary public relation skills, befriended Bilu-da also. As a result he always managed to stock-up the choicest seats for special patrons.

Pandit, too, had his own style in selling tickets. The moment 'House Full' board was hung (which again was Bilu-da's job, more for his height I suppose, for he could reach the hook fixed at the hall entry door with relative ease), Pandit swung into action. He mingled with the crowd and traded his wares with steady but subdued commentaries...

"...First Class – 20 rupees...first class – 20 rupees....Second Class – 15 rupees....second class – 15 rupees... Inter Class – 10 Rupees....Inter Class only 10 Rupees... Third Class 5 Rupees...hurry hurry... only a few tickets left....20 – 15 – 10 – 5 .... Throwaway price...just throwaway price...don't let the full house disappoint you... few tickets...only 20 minutes to main show...."

Soon he would be surrounded by customers like bees around a hive. A demand-dependent bargaining would follow. Once price was negotiated, Pandit would produce the tickets from the folds of his sleeve (for some reasons he never used his pockets for storing his merchandise) hand over the tickets and pocket the cash...

Rarely would Pandit compromise on the price of his merchandise. The price, of course, depended on the popularity of the movie. Pandit never saw the movie, but he had this uncanny ability to assess the shelf life – or should we say the 'house-full-life' of the movies. Accordingly he set the prices, loaded with some 'negotiation' fat – which he would reduce during bargaining, with a standard only-for-you laced submission.

"Only for you sir … I don't want you to go back disappointed…"

"Only for you *Didi* … you came all the way from Hooghly, didn't you?"

"Arre yaar, don't spoil your evening just for a few extra rupees…only for you"

"Hit picture, hit picture… see Dharmendra flatten seven goons with a single punch…special price only for you brother"

Pandit surely knew a thing or two about marketing. He took his business rather seriously. He would not budge on his 'negotiated' price, even to his friends (me included) – but would gladly treat the same friend in Sen-Cabin with a cup of tea or devil chops. He also had a sharp memory, and could generally recognize his patrons whom he had served once. He created a data bank of his patrons in his mind and accordingly mapped their preferences and exploited it craftily.

There was a concrete water tank at the ground level just adjacent to Sen-Cabin which we used as our *dhapi* (a place, usually made of concrete that served as the tryst for male friends, a place for gossiping and smoking. Those days, very rarely would one find a girl in a *dhapi-adda*). Every evening we assembled there, and discussed virtually everything under the sun. However the main topics were girls, politics – mainly Naxal-Police encounter stories – sports and movies, in that order.

Pandit was a mobile encyclopedia on the girls that resided in Hooghly-Chinsurah Municipality area, who ventured to Rupali and Kairi for their weekly quotas of pictures. Sometimes, he even kept tabs on girls who came all the way from Bandel, Chandannagore or even Naihati.

"Tomorrow you will find that fair girl from Kapasdanga in the evening show at Kairi – so Mamu be prepared" – he would say to one of our friends Prasanta – who was more popular as Mamu.

"Which girl?" – Mamu would feign innocence.

"*Arre yaar*, that girl with big bosoms, Mitul, her name, I guess; lives in Kapasdanga, Hooghly. Studies in Balika Bani Mandir, standard eleven. The one you are eyeing for so long"

"Hmmm – and how are you so sure?"

"She is a Soumitra Chatterjee fan. Without fail she would be there on the first Saturday of every new release of Soumitra. Watch out, tomorrow, evening show at Kairi. She would be accompanied by her fat *Boudi* (sister-in-law) – so better be careful, Mamu."

And Mitul would be there with her fat *Boudi* on the following day for the evening show at Kairi…

Ninety out of hundred times, Pandit was correct in his predictions. And by chance if he wasn't, he came up with incredible excuses like – "She must be having her periods" – a wicked grin lacing his *paan*-stained lips.

It was troubled times. Political unrest rocked the whole of Bengal big time. The Naxalites, a communist guerilla group, supportive of Maoist political sentiments and ideologies, became very potent in preaching their ideologies across West Bengal. The party targeted the youth as their cadre. There were some erudite yet firebrand leaders, who could successfully brainwash a large section of the youth – mostly kids from high schools and colleges – into joining and working for the party. The Naxalites chose a quick and radical way of reform. They believed in gunning down and destroying any person or asset they considered supportive of bourgeois-ism. They supported the peasants and lower class tribal group and wanted to overthrow the government and upper classes by force. Later, the Naxal movement spread along the Eastern coast to Odisha, Andhra and Chattisgarh, but it all started in Bengal. The name 'Naxal' was derived from 'Naxalbari' – a small village in the north of West Bengal. Such was the wave of the movement that thousands of students left schools and joined it, without caring for their lives or careers. The aim was to annihilate individual "class enemies" such as landlords, businessmen, university teachers, police officers, politicians of the right and left. The kids were trained to assemble and handle pipe-guns (a country made rudimentary gun made of steel pipes, metal straps and bands for trigger mechanism and fed on homemade 9 mm cartridges packed with gun-powder), homemade bombs and grenades and the likes. Their movements were, naturally, viewed as acts of insurgencies and often we heard of police encounters. Many a young life was lost. Appalling news of deaths, loots, arsons – involving our friends and acquaintances, came so regularly that after a while they lost the element of shock.

However, nobody in our *adda* group was directly involved in this movement. Or so we thought! Our involvement were limited to the gossips and the stories that were rampant, and occasional reading of 'The Red-Books' – which preached theories of Mao Zedong – without much comprehension.

My friendship with Pandit took a curious turn when I was in my tenth standard in Hooghly Collegiate School. I was taller than most boys in our class. I was, should I say rather well built, and also a natural athlete. I say this because I was an automatic choice in my school teams for cricket, soccer and hockey. But life was not all about cricket, soccer, *adda* or movies. We had to study also. Those days, the market was not flooded with professional and specialized coaching centers like what we see today. It was limited to school or college teachers providing private tuitions at nominal fees. The teaching fraternities still believed in the ideology of carving out good students and do their bit in building the nation. For the teachers it was less of business, more of pride. Teachers used to gloat over their pupils' glory – whenever some of their pupils got star marks in their school leaving exams.

I used to bi-cycle to Pradip-da's place near for taking private tuitions in Physics, Chemistry and Maths. Pradip-da was a college-lecturer and lived in Hooghly, near Binodini Girls High School – which was about 3-4 kilometers away from my home. It was at Pradip-da's where I first met Urmi – Urmimala, a tenth standard student of Binodini Girl's High School. She was a fair and slightly plump lass with twinkling eyes which betrayed her serious bespectacled countenance. At some angles, she resembled be-spectacled Indian version of Kate Winslet. She was Pradip-da's neighbour.

I took an instant liking to Urmi, but saw nothing in her behaviour, even after three-four months of taking tuitions together, that suggested even her slightest interest in me.

Girls have this fantastic ability to conceal their emotions pre-relationships, and over-expose and exploit the same post-relationships.

I was trying hard to impress Urmi, but all she had in her mind all the time were studies, studies and only studies. I was not a bad student by any standards, but Urmi was exceptionally good. The only way to impress upon the Urmi-type girls was by bonding oneself physically, chemically and also mathematically to one's subjects and become a nerd! And I was no nerd.

Urmi's world revolved around Physics, Chemistry and Mathematics. Even personalities like Franz Beckenbauer, Bobby Simpson, Boris Spassky, Abebe-Bikila, Mao Zedong, Satyajit Ray, Sean Connory etc failed to create any dents in her cocooned world of Phy-Chem-Maths. The only other thing – or should I say person – that Urmi ever showed slightest interest in was Dev Anand and his movies… I guess all of us have childhood crushes. Dev Anand could have been Urmi's childhood crush!

In our *adda* at the premises of Rupali talkies, soon Urmi became a popular subject of discussion. It became increasingly difficult for me not to bring her topic at least once every evening – a clear evidence of my falling head-over-heels for her. But Urmi never reciprocated or hinted anything to suggest that she was interested in a relationship with me. I was candid enough in admitting that. My friends teased me and also gave all kinds of advice on how to woo Urmi – even though I knew for sure that none in the group had remotest of idea about girls, romance and relationships.

Nikhil was two years senior to us, but studied in the same class for he had failed twice in his term exams. Also, he was the one who supplied us with soft-porn books in Bengali. Books that seemingly taught ignorant readers on the nuances of sex and man-woman relationships! Nikhil came up with suggestions that were outright crass and silly.

"Go, hug her tightly and plant a kiss on her when Pradip-da is not around – and she shall be yours" – Nikhil advised.

"Don't ever do that, because if you do, you will lose her forever" – warned Pandit. "You must wait for the opportune moment, or you must create a situation so that your credibility increases."

"Help her, help her" – advised Poda – "help her with studies, notes, tutorials, whatever."

"That's the problem" – I admitted – "She's a far better student than me. In fact she helps me at every step with those tricky problems that Pradip-da dishes out" – I scratched my head in frustration.

"What are her other areas of interest – apart from studies, that is" – Poda enquired innocuously.

"Correct. Pictures. Is she interested in films? Find out" – Pandit jumped at the cue. Films, after all, were his livelihood. "Find out about her favorite movie star and invite her for movies at Rupali or Kairi."

"Mmmm…interest in films … no not really. But she did talk once or twice about Dev Anand" – I mumbled.

"Great, Dev Anand. The king of romance! I am sure he will help you consummate the romance of your life…. You are in luck bro!" – yelled Pandit.

"Luck?"

"Yes. There is a new Dev Anand – Waheeda Rehman release next Friday. Bilu-da told me Rupali managed a copy of the print for release. Invite her for the next Saturday matinee. Tickets shouldn't be a problem, good old Pandit will manage that" – said Pandit with pride.

Next day at Pradip-da's tuition, with heart in my mouth I managed to put across my preposterous proposal to Urmimala. Would she accompany me for the new Dev Anand – Waheeda Rahman flick for the Saturday matinee? Urmi was stunned, for she never expected such an audacious proposal from me. I licked my lips and waited in pregnant silence for Urmi to respond. Two moments – perhaps three... I heard Urmi reply – "But that's impossible. I have school".

"It's a half-day. School gets over at 12 noon. The show is at 2. What's the problem?"

"My parents won't allow. It's not a children's movie". Those days even a student of standard ten or eleven was only allowed to view patriotic and mythological movies. 'Love' was a cuss word.

"But you are not a child. And you don't have to tell your parents."

Urmi looked at me as if I had just committed the biggest sacrilege in the history of mankind!

"You like Dev Anand, right? Come on, let's enjoy one Saturday afternoon Urmi. The hell won't break loose."

"But what do I tell at home?"

I could sense a hint of acceptance in Urmi's query. I pounced on it.

"Make up a story. Say Pradip-da wants extra classes."

"You are a fool. Pradip-da is our neighbour. Mom will find out in no time."

"Then say you have to go to your friend's place in Chinsurah to collect notes or discuss your project. Make up a story, any story, will you?" I urged.

"Mmmmm....let me think." Urmi was still in two minds.

Urmi continued to keep me in suspense for almost the whole of the week. Finally on Thursday evening, she accepted my proposal. She would take a rickshaw and come directly from school.

On Friday itself I told Pandit about my plans of Saturday. Pandit had once again assured me of the best two seats for the show.

On that momentous Saturday, Poda, Mamu and I arrived at Sen-Cabin directly after school at around twelve thirty. The Dev Anand movie had released the previous day and was running packed house. Pandit and his gang were having a field day.

I was palpably nervous with uncertainties. Would Urmi eventually turn up? Also the adventure of spending three hours in a dark hall in close proximity with the girl that mattered most to me left me fidgety.

Urmi arrived at one-o-clock, in a hooded rickshaw. She paid the fare and sauntered quickly in the relative safety of Sen-Cabin as per my directives. That was the first time I introduced Urmi to the two of my friends – Poda and Mamu. She, too, was clearly nervous. The pink shades on her fair cheeks and tiny beads of perspiration above her lips were not attributable to the heat and humidity alone…

Pandit saw us, but chose not walk into Sen-Cabin. We saw him mingling with the crowd, busy selling tickets in black. The house was full, and the tickets for this Saturday afternoon were in very high demand. I tried to wave at him, but could not manage to establish eye contact. He was busy, twirling in the crowd with his patented muffled commentaries…

"…First Class – 30 rupees…first class – 30 rupees….Second Class – 25 rupees….second class – 25 rupees… Inter Class – 15 Rupees….Inter Class only 15 Rupees… Third Class 10 Rupees…hurry hurry… only a few tickets left….30 – 25 – 15 – 10 …. Throwaway price…you can't afford to miss Dev Anand's actions…hurry hurry…"

Time was ticking fast, and our anxieties were increasing with every passing second. Pandit was supposed to have handed me two first class tickets, here, in Sen-Cabin. But the fellow seemed to be too pre-occupied with his wares today!

At one thirty, I became a nervous wreck. Urmi's incessant pestering on the chances of getting the tickets in hand, and mild threats on getting back home should this uncertainty persist for a little more time were also not helping.

Mamu and Poda also tried to draw Pandit's attention and call him aside for the tickets, but without any success. The bloke was behaving in a funny manner. He was avoiding all our eye contacts and gesticulations. He was too busy selling tickets and bargaining with customers. We could see tickets were selling like hot cakes. Did Pandit keep aside two tickets for Urmi and me, as promised?

Finally at one-forty, I could wait no longer. I trudged down the steps of Sen-Cabin and jostled through the crowd to where Pandit was at business. Poda followed.

"Hey Pandit" – I yelled.

Pandit gave a vacant look. I gesticulated with my upturned palm – where are the tickets, bro?

Pandit gesticulated back, what? Seemingly, he was unable to understand.

I took a few steps forward with Poda closely behind my heels. I went very close to Pandit and asked in a muffled voice,

"Hey Pandit – where are my tickets"

"What tickets?" Pandit questioned back.

"Come on, Pandit. I told you yesterday, didn't I? You were to deliver me two first class tickets in Sen-Cabin".

"Oh that!" – Pandit seemed to remember. "You go there, I am coming" – he ordered.

We came back to Sen-Cabin.

"What happened, you got the tickets or not?" – Urmi was very concerned now. She was glancing at her wrist watch ever too frequently.

"Hang on, we shall make some arrangements" – I said even though I had no plan B in place in the event Pandit did not hand over the promised tickets.

In a while Pandit arrived, perspiring heavily.

"Hey, buddy, where are my tickets?"

Pandit looked at Urmi for a moment. She was visibly uncomfortable. Probably for the first time in her life she was seeing a film ticket blacker within close quarters.

"Look dear" – said Pandit in a business-like tone – "Market is hot. I have only two first class tickets left – you will have to pay fifty rupees for each ticket – so that's a hundred. Agreed?"

"Come on Pandit – that's too heavy for me. You were selling it for thirty rupees there"

"That was some time back. Now rates have gone up."

"Hey, Pandit – what's happened to you? You can't do this to a friend?" – Poda tried to protest.

"Friend? What Friend? You belong to the upper class. And look at me. I am a ticket blacker – a third class rascal with no social status. And you call me a friend! Don't I know our friendship ends right at the boundary walls of this cinema hall. *Saala*. Now come on, shell out hundred rupees or I am going. Time is precious"

Urmi's face contorted in disgust.

"I'm going" – she said. She was visibly upset.

"No wait" – I screamed – and then turned to Pandit and said - "Pandit – are you going to give me the tickets at a fair price or not?"

"Rupees fifty is a very fair price for today bro. This is my *rozi-roti*. Pay or buzz off." Pandit was about to leave.

"Let's go. I am not interested in the film any more" – murmured Urmi.

"No, we will watch the movie" – I hissed. This, now, was a prestige issue. I could never have imagined that Pandit would turn out to be such a turn-coat. I was aghast - all these days I have entrusted and befriended this scoundrel?

"Pandit – one last warning – are you going to give me the tickets at a fair price or not?"

"Leave it. Let's go" – I heard Urmi squeal.

"Well, if I don't what do you think you will do bro? Big deal! Everybody tries a *heropanthi* (to enact a hero) in presence of a girlfriend, eh! Buzz off." – Pandit retorted with a sneer.

That was too much for me to stomach. Blind with rage and humiliation, I pounced on Pandit and held him in a bear hug. Pandit's lean frame could not sustain the impact, and together we rolled down the three steps of Sen-Cabin. My right elbow and knee hurt, but I would not let go of that bastard.

Pandit had his gang. He and his boys were quite used to such street-brawls. I on my side had Poda and Mamu – and collectively between all of us we have not fought a single serious fight in our entire lives. Mamu never left the safe shelter of Sen-Cabin, while Poda followed me with some trepidation, fervently hoping that things do not go out of control. I could see Jagadish-da, the cop, at some distance.

Surprisingly, it was I who had the upper hand in that brawl that day. No sooner we landed on the hard concrete than I sprang up and yanked Pandit up by the collar. And before Pandit or any of his boys could react, I punched him on his face. Pandit took evasive action, but still my punch landed in the corner of his lips and immediately I saw blood splattering out through an ugly gash.

Jagadish-da intervened. Furiously wielding his bamboo stick he first tried to disperse the surrounding crowd and then tried to catch hold of Pandit. But Pandit evaded his clasp, and managed to leap across the wall that separated the two movie halls – Rupali and Kairi – and beat a hasty retreat.

Jagadish-da was sympathetic. He provided some unsolicited advice on why an educated young lad like me should not get entangled in street fights with lowly specimens like Pandit, and escorted me back to Sen-Cabin where Urmi and Mamu were waiting. I could detect a cloud of anxiety on Urmi's fair countenance, now a shade pale from the turn of events.

I had some bruises on my elbows and right knee, where my trousers were torn. Urmi was clearly concerned. At her behest Poda got a bottle of Dettol and wads of cotton from an adjacent chemist's shop. I was pleased that I could overpower a ruffian like Pandit and manage to injure him. I could sense that Urmi was also very pleased with my feat. After all I taught the urchin a lesson or two on how to behave properly! And as she was applying antiseptics on my wounds, I noticed the first sign of relationship budding between Urmi and me; a balmy feeling which easily overpowered the burn caused by the damned antiseptic on my raw bruises!

We ordered for tea and chit-chatted for a while, which centered around Pandit's awkward behavior, and my heroics. After tea, as we were about to leave, Bilu-da came inside, and handed over two tickets to me.

We were puzzled!

How on earth did Bilu-da know that Urmi and I came for the movie?

Jagadish-da trudged in immediately after.

"Go Naru – go, the main movie is about to start" – said Bilu-da in his theatrical accent.

"But how did you know?" – I mumbled.

"Jagadish told me. He said you had some altercation with Pandit?"

"Altercation is an understatement. He had a fight. Don't you see the tell-tale signs?" – boomed Jagadish-da.

"Actually it's Jagadish who retrieved these unsold tickets from Pandit" – said Bilu-da – "Now hurry boy, you wouldn't like to miss the beginning would you? After all in Hindi movies, the main story is wrapped in the first ten minutes and the last ten minutes. The bulk of the time is only songs, music fights and inane comedies, right? Now go." – ordered Bilu-da.

Within a month after that momentous day, Urmi and I got entangled into a serious relationship. It became difficult for us to pass a single day without seeing each other. Rupali and Kairi provided us with the opportunities to get a little physical as well.

A couple of months passed.

One afternoon Urmi and I, with Mamu and Poda in tow came for yet another movie in Rupali; a Bengali detective flick starring Uttam Kumar and Anjana Bhowmick. The movie was mediocre. The denouement was rather long – where, like usual whodunits, all the suspects were rounded off in a room while the hero – Uttam Kumar – ran through the clues and events and zeroed in on the hapless culprit as the heroine watched with star-struck eyes.

After the movie, we walked into Sen-Cabin, where a profoundly more interesting denouement was waiting for us!

We found Bilu-da, Jagadish-da and Pandit having tea and cutlets.

Now this was the last thing we expected. A cop, a ticket-blacker, and a multi-tasking hall employee having a hearty time over evening tea, huh!

"Come, bro, have a cuppa. Namaste *Behenji*, have some *chai*" – Pandit was extremely courteous with folded hands and all!

Urmi was about to leave, when Pandit intervened,

"Arre, don't go away *Behenji* – I may earn my livelihood by selling tickets in black, but I am not that bad a person. Naru is my long time *yaar* – no Naru?"

I was too flabbergasted to show any kind of reaction. This was height of shamelessness.

"What's the meaning of this, Jagadish-da?" I asked. "You are the cop, and you are having tea with this chap here, who openly sells tickets with a premium"

"I am off-duty now brother" – winked Jagadish-da. "Besides, like you, Pandit too is a friend". I could see Bilu-da nodding in agreement.

But my circumspection just won't go. Seeing this, Bilu-da very matter-of-factly said – "The whole thing that happened that Saturday, was a set-up. All of it was Pandit's drama."

"Yes, the whole episode was scripted. We had a meeting the previous evening, and luckily everything went as per plans."

"But that's preposterous! You could have hurt yourself Pandit. That was too much!" – I was still not convinced. I could see Urmi's eyes almost popping out in wonder.

"Oh that's nothing. What's life without little risks? I risk myself every day. I have to, bro. I am not educated like you, *na*?"

"But why did you have to do that?" – It was Urmi who asked softly.

"To create a situation *Behenji*, so that you fall for my friend. I wanted you to discover the hero in Naru! He was so madly in love with you. In our *addas* he would only talk about you. It, kind of, became boring. We had to do something, didn't we?" said Pandit with his usual nonchalance.

Thereafter, we all became friends again. A year and a half passed. In the meantime, Urmi and I frequently visited Rupali and Kairi for movies. And courtesy Pandit and Bilu-da, we always managed to get cozy corner seats. They were the only places where we enjoyed our proximities and covert touches here and there. Why, we even kissed and smooched in the cozy comforts of the dark halls.

Then, one day, Pandit stopped coming to the hall complexes.

Thereafter, we too got busy with our Higher Secondary Exams and the various entrance tests. I managed to get a chance in an Engineering College while Urmi chose to pursue career in Mathematics at the Calcutta University. Our visits to Rupali and Kairi became few and far between, may be once or twice a month.

But not once we saw Pandit. He just seemed to have vanished in the thin air!

There were many stories behind his disappearance. Some said he went back to his village in UP, got married and was busy farming in his ancestral lands. Some said he started his own business in Dwarbhanga. Some said he'd become ascetic and left for the Himalayas in search of Nirvana. But the strongest story which hush-hushed around was that he was eliminated by the police in a covert encounter.

Apparently, selling tickets in black was not Pandit's only vocation. He also stocked pipe-guns, hand grenades and other arms as a middle-man in an arm dealing racket. The arms supply came from Nepal and Bangladesh, and were used in the Naxal movement. He used his exceptional PR skills in the dealings. Not even his closest friends had any wind of his arm-dealing activities. However, once his cover blew, he too was blown to smithereens by the police...

"I risk myself every day..." didn't Pandit say that to me once....

There were many such here-today-gone-tomorrow stories in circulation. Pandit's was just another of those.

I tried to corroborate the encounter story on Pandit's disappearance through Jagadish-da, but he neither agreed, nor denied. Bilu-da, however, strongly believed that Pandit was *encountered.*

We never saw Pandit again...

Time passed. The political unrest in Bengal settled with the insurgency tamed to a point where it lost all its potency and firepower.

As we grew up and graduated, problems started cropping up between Urmi and me.

We discovered we had problems of compatibility. She had her own ideas while I had mine, and we both thought we were right in our stands. Neither of us was ready to budge. It's funny, but small comments that seemed jokes when the relationship was up and running, now appeared as caustic sarcasms.

We met at Sen-Cabin for one last time with hopes to iron out our problems. The meeting turned out to be a disaster. We remained steadfast in our stands. We had tea, even went for a movie, an Uttam-Sabitri family drama which was in its third week in an almost empty house. But even the warm proximity in the near empty hall failed to thaw our relationship.

When we came out of the hall, we both knew it was over. Forever...

This time Pandit was not there to 'create a situation' and mend ours!

THE OWL

The pain was intensifying with every passing moment.

Seething white pain, jack-knifing just above the left rib cage!

Just as it had happened two years back in Bhusawal…

What do I do now? Do I wake Neha up? Do I ask for a glass of water?

By my side, Neha, my wife, was sleeping peacefully. I could feel the tremors of her soft snores. Her face, only partially visible, was filled with divine innocence. Her sleeping countenance was bound to invoke sympathy. She was like incarnation of Maya… Nah – let her sleep. In any case, now I could sense that the pain was easing a little…

On that eventful night in Bhusawal, when I was in deep distress it wasn't Neha…I had Milu by my side. Milu had woken up on her own. Somehow, even in her sleep, she'd come to know about my discomfort! She'd gotten up with a jolt and asked, "What's happened? Are you okay? Do you need some water?"

From Bombay we had taken the train to Nagpur. I was going on a business trip, while Milu – Mrs Mila Sharma – was going to cover some event for the newspaper for which she worked. We often managed to travel together. Necessity is the mother of invention – they say. For our own sakes, it was then necessary for both of us to spend nights together. So somehow we managed to schedule our tours together. On that eventful night, we'd got to know through a public announcement at Bhusawal that there would be an inordinate delay due to some derailment. We took a snap decision to get down at Bhusawal and spend the night together in a hotel.

Mila was the wife of my friend Sudhin. She was a journalist. Economic independence begets an aura of arrogance in females. For Mila, this was far more than plain arrogance. Her care-a-damn attitude towards all social norms led her eventually, what public would label,to cross promiscuity. And I loved it. Somehow, it was very befitting to Mrs Mila Sharma's character. She used to treat Sudhin as a non-entity. Sudhin, without doubt, was naïve, but that he was completely ignorant of our relationship is something I would never vouch for! I thought he *pretended* ignorance. Whether this was because he was afraid of scandals, or because he was scared of his wife, or was it because of his obsession towards Mila so that she doesn't walk out on him one can never say… No man worth his salt would have tolerated his wife screwing around with another guy, but incredible as it may sound, Sudhin did.

I had no complaints though. I took full advantage of this and savored every moment with Mila. If a man's liking had any connections to the curves of a dangerously attractive woman, I liked Mila. She was attractive, voluptuous, and had the right curves. Added to this was the element of zing that I thought was always present in such extra-marital relationships. It was like the over-fermented toddy in the winter afternoons, sour and tangy. Milu, on her part, had many explanations to justify this relationship like, before meeting me she never knew the real taste of true love, that her husband was incapable of loving... blah... blah... blah. God alone knew what she meant by Sudhin was *incapable,* because outwardly, there was nothing wrong with him. Physically that is. And I often wondered why was necessary for her to give any reasons at all - I had never asked for any explanations. My intent was to enjoy her company...to enjoy *her* to be precise, and I was happy to have her with frequent regularity. Milu, too, had her needs. She made herself available at the drop of a hat. Our *coincidental* business trips dragged us together to Hyderabad, Bangalore, Madras, Pune... at regular intervals.

Whenever Milu talked of love, it irritated me all ends up. 'Love' in her lingo was like a nickel-plated metal – fake, cheap and vulgarly glossy. All it would require is a few light taps before the gloss started chipping off. But I did well to conceal my feelings, because I did not want to invite Milu's wrath. I was very scared of Milu's ire. For that matter, I was very scared of any woman's ire. Keep them in good humour, use them, enjoy them and then at an opportune moment, dump them!

But love or no love – I must confess, I was a trifle moved by Milu's behaviour that night when the pain struck me for the first time... How on earth did the fast-asleep Milu come to know that I was having some difficulty in breathing? No, it wasn't just breathing, it was pain. White-hot-pain cutting through my left rib cage, like a sheath knife...

Pain – agony – anguish ... is that what Milu had experienced when she first heard of my marriage?

With a sardonic smile she'd said, "Wish you a long and happy married life."

Through the imperceptible tremor in Milu's lips I could sense the Armageddon... I could see the Doomsday through her eyes brimming with humiliation....

Did Milu love me? Was there ever a moment when love in her mind had overpowered the lust for me? For the first time I wasn't so sure...

I could clearly see the dark shadows of curse under her shimmering eyes... but by then I'd already given my commitments to Neha...

Now, again I sensed the pain that had abated for a while shooting up my rib cage up into the small of my throat… almost paralyzing me… yet I was in my senses… I could still vividly remember the last letter that Milu wrote… every line of it …

"I can never forget you! Seven years, yes the memories that I have gathered trough the past seven years – the sheer volume of it -- will always keep you alive and kicking within me. I can sense you everywhere, in every little thing. I still feel the thrill flowing through my veins. Can you think of a place where we did not do it? Hotel Horizon… at your friends empty apartment in Ahmedabad… in my bedroom… at your place on the kitchen-floor on the day your maid servant did not turn up… in the numerous shower-rooms… on the dining table… on the damp grass at the Lodhi Gardens on that wintry evening… at the lodge in Shantiniketan… in the cramped rear seat of your Maruti… at the hotel in Bhusawal when we had suddenly decided to abandon our journey to Nagpur…

Tell me, is it humanly possible to forget all these? I sincerely wish I suffered a loss of memory for they shall stifle me, bit by bit, for all the remaining moments that I live. Who ever said memories were sweet? Bullshit.…

For you, of course, it's going to be different … at least for the time being. The thrills of your new life will cloud your memories for a while. But, honestly tell me dear, can you ever eradicate me out of your mind for ever.…?" Oh yeah, Milu wrote good prose, I must admit. She was a journalist after all…

Armageddon…. Doomsday.…what the fuck was happening to me…?

The breathlessness was benumbing… I could almost feel a vacuum in my bosom… does one have a similar feeling after being gutted…? Is this the agony of hell-fire…?

Did Milu -- Mrs Mila Sharma – experience a similar feeling when I'd dumped her? Did Sudhin Sharma undergo similar sensation after he discovered about the affair between his wife and his best pal?

Sudhin was my schoolmate. In college, too, we were together. His affair with Milu blossomed and gelled right in front of my eyes. An affair that had started slowly, took its time to ripen and then slowly culminated into a marriage. It was almost like the formation of a dome. Only it was a termite dome … Milu and Sudhin's marriage that is. Outwardly, a solid hillock-like appearance, inside it was all porous and puffy, with colonies of white termites wriggling nauseatingly.

Sudhin, somehow, was always very helpful towards me. As a matter of fact, I also got my first job through Sudhin. But I daresay, I could never really understand my friend.

I still remember the evening when Sudhin came back to his apartment, unannounced. He was flying to Calcutta to cover some Film Festival. But his flight was cancelled in the last minute due to some mechanical snag or whatever. He came back late in the evening and found me with Milu in their apartment. Yet, nonchalantly, he asked, "Oh, it's you," and that was it! Now how would one define his reaction? Was it just a facade of generosity, or was it sheer hell-I-care attitude towards his wife? How generous, how unconcerned can a person be?

"He came to see you," Milu had replied – not that Sudhin was expecting any reply – "It was pretty late, so I asked him to stay the night."

"Oh", said Sudhin without much ado, and went off to the bathroom for a wash. How could Sudhin accept such a ludicrous reason from his wife? How much peace loving, how uninvolved can a mere mortal be?

Even after all that, Sudhin kept our friendship intact. Didn't Sudhin, even for a moment, feel a pang of jealously? Did Sudhin at all have love left for Mila? Or was he actually pleased to see his best friend satiate his wife?

I glanced at Neha – my wife, still sleeping like a baby...

I shall never emulate the apathetic Sudhin. I will love Neha. She was my wife after all. I will, consciously and subconsciously, leave my past behind and wholeheartedly love my wife. I will love her like no husband ever loved his wife. I will never allow Neha to realize agony... Pains... are very painful!

A flash of pain darted up my left ribcage, like a ripple of sheet lightening. Oh no, it's suddenly getting worse. I could sense that I was choking. Neha... Neha get up. How come you are sleeping so peacefully when your husband is in distress? Neha, I promise, ours is going to be a successful marriage. I promise. We will prove that our marriage was indeed made in heaven. Oh come on, wake up Neha, I need help.... I am unable to breathe Neha... I am unable to talk... Milu... Milu would have woken up..sheonce did, you know...I can feel Milu's presence here... Milu rebuking me... ridiculing me - "I am ashamed of myself. I thought you were never interested in marriage, so I had often requested you not to marry, ever. Remember, I had even proposed we spend the rest of our lives like this... and like an idiot, so many times I had confessed that I was never going to live without you…how damned foolish of me!"…oh Neha don't you hear, Milu is here for retribution…

I mustered the last of my energy reserves and managed to nudge Neha…

Neha moved a little and opened her eyes. As soon as she saw me she sat up with a jolt. That was understandable. I was sure that with the intense pain, my countenance assumed that of Coppola's old, haggard, Count Dracula. Neha muffled a scream and said, "What's happened? Are you okay? Do you need some water?" The exact words that Mrs. Mila Sharma had uttered in that hotel room in Bhusawal. I was not impressed. What I needed then was more than water…

Neha bent down and touched my forehead, and very tenderly asked, "Tell me darling, what's happened, what's bothering you?" I could feel her soft breasts on my chin. I tried to tuck my face inside the velvety comfort of her breasts. I did not need water… I needed love… I needed life… I tried my best to speak even though I realized that all I could manage was gibberish groans… "Neha, I will love you… I will love you with all my life… you will never be unfulfilled in any way… you will never experience any pain… pains, Neha, pains are very painful….no Neha, never…"

***

They made wild love for the second time that evening.

Rajat rolled over and lit a cigarette, puffing silently. For full five minutes, they spoke nothing, savoring the languid togetherness. Then, Neha, running her fingers through Rajat's hairy chest, said, "Well, I'm glad everything went off peacefully."

Rajat gave one last drag on his cigarette, dispatched the butt with a deft flick of fingers into the dark exterior and said, "Yeah. Getting a direct divorce these days is so fucking difficult. It would've taken ages, I'm sure. So tell me, Neha, when are we going to legalize our relationship?"

Neha grinned mirthfully, as if she just heard the joke of this millennium. She rolled over on Rajat's torso and said,

"Come on Rajat. You must learn to be a little patient. I can't marry now. Not at least for the next few months. What would everybody say? After all, my husband died of a heart-attack only fifteen days ago."

Rajat thought for a while and said,

"Tell me Neha, don't you have *any* feelings for that person?"

"Feelings? For that scoundrel?" Neha got up, feral and wild like an untamed mare, and walked across to the chair where her clothes were lying in a heap.

"But you married him Neha; willfully. You are still his legal widow."

"I know. I was fully aware of all his activities, his past, his properties, his everything, before I agreed to marry him."

From his reclining posture, Rajat sat up on the bed and said,

"You mean you knew everything before you married him?"

"Of course," said Neha. She had just managed to drape her nakedness with a saari. Now as she twirled around admiring her saree-clad curves on the dressing table mirror she said,

"Do you know Mila? Mila Sharma; the journalist friend of mine? She had had a torrid affair with that man. She had once cautioned me about him. Womanizing was his only hobby. He also had developed a debilitating heart disease and was on continuous medication. He was advised a bypass surgery by his doctors. But I persuaded him against it." Neha slowly walked towards the open window. A barn-owl, which had taken refuge in the window sill, flew off with some ugly hoots.

"But how were you so sure that he was going to die?" Rajat asked.

"I had a talk with his doctor. His heart condition was precarious. But you are right, even a precarious heart condition does not guarantee any time frame on one's death. But it happened, didn't it?" Neha paused.

"What if it had not happened?" Rajat could see Neha's profile looming murkily in the semi-darkness, gentle breeze playing with some loose strands on her forehead.

Neha did not immediately reply. After a long silence she said, "I made sure it happened. I replaced his prescribed drugs with some innocuous pills. Ever since our marriage he relied solely on me for his medicines. He never had a clue that he was not having his life saving drugs. It was just a matter of time before he had the attack. I only had to make sure that once he had an attack, it was fatal. So that night, when he had the attack, I pretended to sleep."

"You mean, you knew?" Hissed Rajat in astonishment..

Neha turned towards Rajat. The fully developed moon formed a devilish halo behind her innocent face.

"All along" she said –"while he was writhing in pain I was feigning sleep… for two long hours…until he shook me up".

"And then?" asked Rajat, breaking the ghostly silence. At that instant the power went off, engulfing the entire room in darkness, save for the dispersed moonlight behind Neha's face, her body silhouetting against the pale moonlight…

Rajat could hear, Neha replying in a voice of an enchantress … "after I woke up I made sure he suffered his way to the end without any medication or aid… until he was *found* dead the next morning…"

Rajat could hear the hoot yet again…the owl was seeking a refuge…

***

ORC 4851

SILIGURI

I still remember the registration number of the vehicle. A shining black Ambassador – Mark I model.

My Dadu (maternal grandpa) was a Government civil contractor, operating mainly in the north of West Bengal. All his projects were in and around Jalpaiguri and Darjeeling districts. So much so, he'd set up his permanent camp in Siliguri, and then after a few years built a house by the highway connecting New Jalpaiguri and Siliguri.

Many civil structures in the region had a stamp of my Grandpa's handicraft! For example the entire superstructure of the New Jalpaiguri station, including the platforms, over-bridge, station building, car park, portico – everything – was built under Dadu's supervision. I am not very sure whether he worked on an EPC (Engineering, Procurement and Construction) basis, or he was just a constructor. He was a civil engineer. I often saw him going through blueprints – those days all engineering drawings were on blue ammonia prints – and calculations. So he was, in a way, involved right from the Engineering stage of the projects. Also he had in his fleet three trucks – all privately registered – which used to ply with steel, stone-chips, cement bags and other construction material, and a massive road roller.

Besides Dadu owned a spanking new Ambassador car – ORC 4851, which he used for his own commuting.

North Bengal, those days, was our summer abode. Almost every summer holiday, my Dida (maternal grandma) would travel to Siliguri with me and my little sister.

One fine morning, on one such summer breaks, we alighted from Darjeeling Mail at the New Jalpaiguri station. The construction work was nearing completion. The platform bore tell-tale signs of fresh concrete work. The woodwork on the over-bridge and the lamp posts still smelled of fresh paint. The station building was getting the first coat of white primer.

But Dadu wasn't there to receive us! We were a little worried, but Dida, the strong lady that she was, hired a porter and we trudged out of the station building into the newly paved car-park.

And lo and behold! Dadu was there, leaning on a shiny black Ambassador and merrily puffing at his cigarette – and all the while trying to conceal a hint of a victorious grin that had how-was-the-surprise written all over. Purposely,

Dadu had not disclosed Dida about the car to surprise her, and came up triumphs.

I can never forget Dida's childlike mirth at that instant! In modern day, I am sure, she would've then and there embraced her husband and planted an impulsive kiss on his cheek, but fifty years ago such an act was unthinkable. Those days people were wired to clothe even their behavioral spontaneities. But the glitter in her eyes betrayed her emotions. It was a mix of surprise and deep, deep love for Dadu. My Dadu-Dida was a very lovey-dovey couple. But that is not the topic of this story, even though love plays a very pivotal role in its denouement...

I am talking of my love for the black Ambassador! I had fallen for her, instantly.

Shankar was the chauffeur – a scrawny malnourished chap – who, most probably, hailed from Bihar and spoke broken Bengali. I addressed him as Shankar-da.

Who said children are innocent? I was just about seven or eight years old then, but my devious mind told me that my gateway to gain access to the car was to befriend Shankar-da, ASAP.

Hitherto, my car ride experience was only limited to those yellow and black taxis in Calcutta (those days it wasn't Kolkata) – mostly ill maintained, smoke spewing jalopies with torn upholstery; that too, once in a blue moon, when we visited Calcutta. In contrast, ORC 4851 was akin to a Rolls Royce. Whenever the car was parked, I sat behind the wheels and fiddled with the steering, gear-shift lever and the steering mounted horn – much to the chagrin of Shankar-da. I had to get down from the driver's seat to reach the foot-controls; the brake, clutch and the accelerators. I liked to watch the dashboard and those blinking lights in the dials therein, which sprang to life as soon as the ignition key was inserted. And my little mind was flooded with queries. All kinds of queries – and all related to the car...

- Why is the pedal on the extreme right oblong shaped while the other two are squares?
- Why does the car does 'vroom vroom' when the oblong pedal is pressed?
- What is a neutral?
- Why do you have to change gears so frequently?

- How is the engine rotating the wheels, that too sometimes forward sometimes reverse?

I bombarded my questions to Shanker-da regularly, as I played with the various controls in the car.

Little did I know that Shankar-da was only a driver, not an automobile engineer or even a qualified mechanic? He knew little about the technicalities of a car. For example, he told me that I had to first press the clutch – the pedal on extreme left – to shift the gear, but failed to explain why. He knew gear changing was essential as the car accelerated or slowed down, but couldn't satisfactorily explain why. Else the car would stop – was his standard answer.

Even at that age I wasn't fully satisfied with his explanations, yet my questions kept effervescing out with alarming frequency…

Whenever Dadu was at home, for afternoon lunch break or in the evening, I ran to the car park and sat behind the wheel. Nothing else in the world was more entertaining for me than fiddling with the car controls.

Then one day, I asked Shankar-da to teach me how to drive.

The fact that even my feet didn't reach the foot controls was not deterrent enough for me to muster courage and propose my preposterous request. My enthusiasm to drive the machine superseded all logic.

Shankar-da was aghast! Anybody in true sense would have been aghast by the sheer ludicrousness of my demand. He disregarded my request almost immediately with an air of authority. But I wasn't the one to give up so easily. From then on, with renewed zeal, day after day, I started pestering Shankar-da for driving lessons.

Shankar-da came up with many excuses:

- You won't be able to drive *Khokababu*…
- Why don't you understand, you are not even tall enough to reach the brakes…
- You first have to grow up; I promise I will teach you once you grow up…
- If your Dadu comes to know he will be very cross…
- I may even lose my job…

But with every refusal, my determination became doubly tenacious. I kept on egging Shankar-da to accede to my request. Only it wasn't a request any more, it was a demand.

At long last, one afternoon, Shankar-da budged, more to get me off his back than anything else.

He made me sit in front of him, with only my hands on the wheel, while we went for a spin. All the while Shankar-da kept praying that nobody sees us! But as Edward Murphy had said – "if anything can go wrong – it will" – Ramesh-da spotted us. Ramesh-da was the driver of the road-roller, a big burly man with a kind face. As a matter of fact when the car wasn't available I spent time on the road-roller to hone up my technical curiosity on automobiles. But it did not excite me as much. The steel steering just wouldn't rotate when the roller was static. Also the dashboard – if one can call the rudimentary meters on a road-roller a dashboard that is – was not at all glitzy. Anyway, after a short drive on the adjacent highway, as we were entering our compound, Ramesh-da saw us. In no time the matter went up to Dadu. More than me, Shankar-da became the focus of Dadu's ire. He was admonished for his crass irresponsibility. And that marked the end of my driving adventures – at least for then.

CHINSURAH

Few years later, probably I was in the tenth or eleventh standard, Dadu retired and came to live at Chinsurah for good. All of us, Dida in particular, were very happy. Dadu was a foodie, and Dida was a great cook. Whether Dadu turned foodie because of Dida's culinary skills or Dadu's love for food forced Dida to become a great cook, I do not know, but what I know for sure is that they complemented each other. Dadu loved to visit the vegetable and fish market daily, something I hated all my life, while Dida loved to cook to perfection and feed Dadu, and of course, us.

However, I had one more reason for being happy. ORC 4851!

While Dadu had sold off all his other vehicles, he'd brought the black ambassador along with him. I was delighted to notice that all these years couldn't take the sheen off the black machine. She was at her elegant best!

The moment I saw her, I itched to sit behind the wheels and take her for a round. I was in my adolescence, grown adequately tall to reach the foot-controls easily. But the incident in Siliguri was etched deeply in my mind, which prevented me from asking Ashok-da to help me learn driving.

Ashok-da was the new chauffeur. He was a soft spoken, medium built man with a rather thick moustache that was misfit on his narrow countenance. He had sunken cheeks and prominent cheek bones. He was about 25-26 years of age and was nice and friendly with me. We discussed contemporary films and of course, the car. I found him more knowledgeable than Shankar-da – as far as technicalities of automobiles are concerned. But secretly I was deeply jealous of Ashok-da. I used to see the metal disc of the key-ring that held the car's ignition key dangling from Ashok-da's trouser pocket (for some reason he always flaunted that) and wished fervently that it dangled from my pocket instead of his.

Apart from my deep interest for the car, there was one more compelling reason for me to quickly learn driving.

Mukta and Alpana were two lasses who lived in the neighbourhood. They went to a different school than where I went, for mine was a boys-only school (something which I regret till date, why couldn't I have gotten a chance to study in a co-ed school?), but we were in the same standard. Mukta was tall, slim and fair with small eyes with a hint of Mongoloid feature, while Alpana was slightly short with a tendency of plumpness. I am sure wherever she is today, she has put on a lot of weight and is enjoying her life as a cuddly Mom or even a Grand-Mom, who knows? Her skin was dark but glowing and her face was endowed with big bright eyes that always sparkled whenever we crossed path. Or so I'd liked to imagine! There was only one thing common to them. Both were damned pretty. And I dreamt of dating them both! We mixed as friends, shared storybooks and vegetarian jokes, sometimes discussed contemporary Bengali films and novels – nothing beyond that. I could never muster courage to ask them for a date, which in those days was limited to a matinee show and chewing *mungphalis* (peanuts) in the interval, perhaps an accidental covert touch here and there.

I'd be lying if I didn't say that all the while I was looking for an opportunity to impress them so that they go head over heels for me. I often dreamt that they – or at least one of them – will be in distress and I'd arrive as the savior prince in a shiny armor. But in reality, in those days, domesticated damsels were seldom in distress, and even if they were, being there at the right time to help them was a one-in-a-million chance.

In ORC 4851 I found a unique prop to impress and influence Mukta and Alpana. I was sure they'd vie to date me if one day I managed to drive past them in that mean-machine! But that was not to be. I could never ask Ashok-da to give me a lesson in driving – something I'd easily done to Shankar-da when I was a kid. I guess, as we grow up and lose our innocence, our minds get clogged with guilt and hesitation. As we acquire worldly knowledge, we also jam our thoughts with sloth and trepidation.

Geeta-di used to work as our household help. There was a small room in our terrace where she stayed. She was just about older to me by two or three years, but had a well-developed body. She was slightly bucktoothed, but was blessed with good endowment and curves. I would be lying if I said that I never cast covert glances on her rather shapely curves.

She, too, was quite pally with me. Once in a while she would go for Bengali movies in the matinee show, and would without fail, narrate me the storyline and share her opinions on the quality of the film.

Then, one quiet summer afternoon, I discovered Geeta-di and Ashok-da in a compromising position. An incident that changed my life forever!

I had afternoon classes, and was expected to return only around 4 pm. But for some reason, most probably the teacher himself was absent; I came back at around 2:30.

The main door at the ground floor was unlocked. Something was amiss! The car was in the garage. I stealthily entered and found Ashok-da's sandals near the shoe-rack in the ground floor.

Something warned me to maintain stealth. I knew Dadu and Dida were having their post lunch siesta in the first floor. I pussyfooted up the stairs straight to the second floor terrace room, which Geeta-di occupied.

I discovered Geeta-di with her disheveled saari and her blouse unhooked, exposing her ample breasts. Ashok-da sprang back as I appeared from behind. Geeta-di stared at me in horror while trying to hide her modesty with her hands.

I too was shaken, my legs trembling. That was the first time I was exposed to a sexual intimate scene between a man and a woman. In pre-internet, even pre-VCR days, x-rated films were virtually non-existent. My exposure to such steamy stuff, up until then, was zero. Suddenly I had an unexpected live exposure. It had never occurred to me that Ashok-da and Geeta-di could have a relationship. The incident had a lasting effect on me, but not too long lasting, because of a reason!

However, the incident tore our friendships apart. Uneasiness, like a suffocating pall of smoke, hung around the three of us, and each of us started avoiding the other. I don't know what transpired between Ashok-da and Geeta-di thereafter, but Geetadi could not look straight into my eyes (nor was I able to do that for some reason) while Ashok-da started avoiding me big time. We had a verandah in the ground floor which had a wooden bench. If he wasn't driving – which was seldom in the small sleepy town of Chinsurah – he used to laze around on the bench. I joined him there, and we talked. But after that incident, if I went there, he left immediately and went to the garage, into the car. If I went anywhere near the car, he came back to the verandah.

I genuinely wanted to forget everything and get back to talking terms, both with Ashok-da and Geeta-di, but that was not to be.

A month passed. Summer was at its peak. Finally one day, as I got back from tuitions and was parking my bicycle, Ashok-da walked to me and with some trepidation said,

- Err..umm…I have a request…if only you care to listen…
- Hmmm – I responded, anticipating what was coming.

- I plea you to forget about what happened between Geeta and me, you know what I mean…and …and I want this secret to be buried forever…we don't want this to be known…you understand, right? I could see genuine remorse in Ashok-da's eyes.

I looked at Ashok-da for a moment, perhaps two and then said,

- Will you give me driving lessons, Ashok-da?

To date, I do not know what made me say so at that very moment. Blackmailing was not even remotely in my mind. As a matter of fact, I was still unaware of what blackmailing was. The truth is, telling everybody about the indecent incident was never in my agenda. Also, if Ashok-da refused to give me driving lessons, I would have never gone on to tell the sleazy story to the world with any malicious intent. (I am doing it now, though – but this is purely for the sake of the story, also I do not consider the incident sleazy anymore. For me, it was a natural denouement to a situation when a relationship was developing and a young couple found themselves all alone in a quiet summer afternoon. My intent is not malicious even now, it never was.)

Ashok-da readily acceded to my request.

From that day, every afternoon Ashok-da and I would hit the deserted roads with ORC4851. Only this time I was behind the wheels, deeply engrossed in Ashok-da's lessons.

Soon I mastered the art of driving a car – or so I thought until one day I saw Mukta and Alpana on the street while I was driving.

That day Ashok-da was giving me a lesson on reversing.

- Remember, when you steer left – the car veers left, and when you steer right the car goes right – this is true for reverse as well. Okay?
- Okay – I said. By then I was confident that it was going to be a breeze.
- So now imagine you forgot something, and you will have to go back home to pick it up. Now on this narrow road you cannot have a full turning radius. So you will have to take half turn to the right, reverse to the left, then again take half more turn to the right till the car has reversed its direction, right? Ashok-da was quite articulate, I must say!
- Okay sir.

I took half a turn on the road and immediately spotted my girls on my right. Mukta and Alpana were returning from some tuition class, their canvas bags slung on their shoulders. We, boys, used to commute on bicycles, but girls, generally, walked or took cycle rickshaws.

Mukta and Alpana spotted me behind the wheels. Now this was the moment I was waiting for. I was on cloud nine, in an instant. Which one's gonna propose me first? – I started contemplating. I saw them veering left and walking past the rear of my car. I could see them in the rear view mirror.

- Ok now engage the reverse gear and slowly veer left as you move backwards; keep an eye on the mirrors though. I heard Ashok-da's voice.

I engaged the reverse gear. I saw the girls in the rear view mirror, and suddenly something happened to me. I pressed the accelerator pedal and released the clutch with a jerk – something which I shouldn't have done after all the trainings. Was it concentration lapse, or was it due to show off? I actually wanted to show the girls that I was an expert driver. Most times, mis-synchronisation of releasing the clutch and pressing the throttle causes the car to stop with a jerk – but as ill luck would have it, this time the car bolted back. And before Ashok-da could insert his leg between mine to apply the break, the machine groaned, sped back and the rear wheels got stuck in a drain, spinning violently. The rear protruding bumper behind the boot rammed against a brick wall with a sickening thud, and immediately created a gaping hole exposing the garden behind. But the worst thing that happened was the plight of the girls! Both Mukta and Alpana escaped by the proverbial hair's breadth, but in an attempt to evade my rogue car, backpedalled into the drain; both of them. Along with their bags and books, that is. Their friendship remained united even in their falls!

Ashok-da was dumbfounded. So was I. And I was equally distressed. I wasn't sure whether the cause of my distress was due to the broken wall and the dented bumper, or the fall of my girls in the drain or my fall in their eyes and hearts!

I helped Mukta and Alpana out of the drain. Save for some minor bruises, they were okay, physically that is. And they were seething! I tried to mumble some apologies which were thundered down by their screams. I offered to take them to a doctor, which was rejected with supreme haste and loud denials. My girls just wanted to get back home with vows that they would never to see my face again…

Surprisingly, we managed to keep the incident low key. The matter never reached Dadu. I *pataoed* (cajoled) Dida and managed to extract five hundred rupees for the compensation to the owner of the garden for which the garden wall was damaged, and another five hundred for repair of the dent, which Ashok-da managed through his known car repair shop.

The best part was that even after this incident, Ashok-da continued to give me driving lessons, until I acquired confidence to drive alone on busy roads. Mukta and Alpana became friends again. Many a times thereafter, we relived the incident in our discussions, and had hearty laughs. But our relationships never got beyond clean friendship. Neither Mukta nor Alpana showed any special considerations for me for my newly acquired skills. But Ashok-da and Geeta-di's relationship culminated into a marriage.

Soon, I crossed 18 and I acquired my license, and fulfilled my dream to lord over ORC 4851.

I became an expert driver.

Thank you Geeta-di.

Thank you Ashok-da.

But for you, I could have never fulfilled my dream!

***

BROWN AND GREY

I got acquainted with William 'Billy' Brown when I was fifteen…

Those were the days when there was no internet, no mobile phones, no computers, nothing. Only means of communication was through letters. And there were black mechanical telephones, which only allowed ten percent of its calls to go through. They were regarded more as mere show pieces in living rooms than as useful and effective means of communication.

Compared to the present day, the communication system – or rather the lack of it - was a major hindrance towards connecting and communicating with the members in the opposite sex.

Billy had reached an age when ninety percent of his mind, like any fifteen-year-adolescent, was occupied with thoughts of dames for ninety-five percent of his time. In his friend's circle girls were the main topic of discussions. So, naturally, even without an effective aid of communication, he was aware of histories and geographies of all girls in the neighbourhood and beyond…

Cursory exchange of glances was often mistaken as the blossoming of an affair. Hours were spent on street corners with hopes that 'she' would come out of her cocoon to visit the nearby bookstore for stationeries. His slow-cycling skills had improved by following girls to their schools as they walked.

All this, despite the fact that none of the efforts actually bore fruits! The glances were more out of scorn than sympathy. The 'she' barely noticed him during her visits to the bookstore or the chemist, and also while walking to her school…

He got frustrated, but had not lost hopes. He started looking for more and more options. There was no dearth of girls, only there were no means to effectively communicate except letters. But letters were too risky. Notwithstanding the risk, in desperation, he tried to slip in a letter or two in the letter boxes and in the process once almost got beaten up by the security guards. It was needless to say he never got answers to any of his letters…

And then one day, in a magazine, he discovered Molly, Molly Ray.

Molly, based in Howrah, was looking for pen friends. There were many ads for pen-friend columns, but somehow, Molly's name caught his attention…

He started imagining how Molly looked. Was she fair or dusky, slim or plump, heavy or light bosomed, her buttock was apple shaped or pear shaped?

Soon, in his imagination, he pictured Molly as buxom and attractive lass, and immediately, she transformed into the girl of his dreams.

I too saw the pen-friend ad. Needless to say, I too, was attracted by the name. Without wasting time, I wrote my first letter to Miss Molly Ray, proposing her pen-friendship. By then I had realized, having a real girlfriend was never going to be easy, so might as well get one through letters...

Little did I know, that even through letters, it wasn't going to be easy? The turn-around time for a reasonably prompt reply in those days was around seven to ten days. So from the sixth day onwards, I became fidgety, every now and then running to the post box expecting a reply.

Meanwhile on day five, Billy Brown wrote his first letter to Molly, pleading her to be his pen-friend.

On day twenty, Billy Brown got a reply from Molly Ray accepting him as her pen-friend. On the other hand I knew that Miss Ray was never going to respond to my letter. It was a setback but it eventually sunk in me that I was in the rejection list of Molly Ray...

The friendship between Molly and Billy continued to flourish, even though it only bordered around flirtatious innuendos and never culminated in an affair.

Soon, Billy and Molly passed their high schools, and got busy into building their respective careers. Exchange of letters dried up, and after Billy left his home for a residential Engineering College, it stopped altogether. Molly Ray was lost in the sands of time...

***

Billy Brown did his mining engineering and got into a reasonably good job immediately after. After six years, at the age of twenty nine he got married to a girl who was chosen by his parents. He never studied in a co-ed school, and in his branch of engineering – Mining - there were no girls. At his job place also, there were no lady co-workers. So for him it had been an all-male environment all along. His wife was the first woman he ever touched and kissed, exactly the way things were scripted for Indian boys.

In due course, Billy got a kid, bought a flat and got nicely settled in life. Looking for better opportunities, he switched jobs four or five times, rose to a reasonably senior level, and then one day retired from a MNC at the age of sixty two.

Times changed. This was an era of smart phones and internet, where an overdose of information-flow is the order of the day. Diarrhea of information flowed through emails, text messages, whatsapp, calls, TVs, newspapers, live blogs, Facebook, twitter, virtually from everywhere … eventually pressurizing every individual to coup with just reading and replying.

But Billy was far from being pressurized. The only email contacts that he had were official. So post retirement, with his official email id liquidated, he lost all email contacts. He was never into Facebook and twitter. He wasn't even sure how to open a Facebook account!

So, post retirement, Billy tried his hands at gardening, but his aged back did not agree. He was never into reading, yet he tried to read novels. His wife was an avid reader. The first book he started upon his wife's recommendation – "Gone with the wind" – he could complete only forty pages. His wife recommended detective stories. He tried that too. Sherlock Holmes could not excite him. Miss Marple couldn't entice him. He changed genres; from crime, to thriller, to comedy, to soft love stories, to horror, to biographies … nothing could keep him awake beyond ten pages…

Mrs. Brown went to work. Their son lived independently in Pune. So, Mr. Brown was all alone throughout the day knowing not what to do. All these years he had only one hobby – his work. While he was still working, he struggled for time. It was the most precious commodity of his life. Suddenly, post retirement, time became his biggest enemy… He eagerly waited for his wife to return from work. But on most days, his wife was very tired. Also, after she was back, she had to do all the household chores. This left the wife with a dour mood. She simply did not have the energy to chat with Mr. Brown. This left Billy more frustrated. Their sex life anyway had trickled down to may be once in two months, like ritualistic drills. Now even the chats were drying up.

Inevitably, this led to a few quarrels. Mr. Brown grumbled about his wife not giving him adequate time. Mrs. Brown irritatingly countered by saying she'd had a hard day, and she was tired … the usual tiffs that are seen in most households.

This left Billy more and more frustrated.

Then one day, his son came on a weekend. He, too, was more interested in chatting on his smartphone with friends, miles apart, than chatting with his father, sitting across in the sofa! What was so interesting in chats through phones? – wondered Billy. So he asked his son who smiled, finished his chat, and said,

"Are you in Facebook papa?"

"No, what's so great about it?"

"It's a social networking platform. You can connect with your friends, relatives, colleagues, anybody, right here from where you are sitting and get to know every little details of who's doing what through posts."

"Can you connect to old, long lost friends?"

"Of course, only if they have a Facebook account. You can also share photos and videos. You can share your feelings, your status, your joy, your sorrows … everything."

"Hmmm…" – said Billy.

His mind suddenly started racing. Molly Ray! Instantly, Molly's imaginary figure, which he had built while he was at school, sprang before his mind's eye. Will Molly be available in the Facebook? How would he recognize her, he'd never even met her or exchanged photos. They had communicated only through letters.

"How'd you recognize long lost friends, say a school friend whom you never met in all these years. He must've changed quite a bit" – asked Billy, now a little more curious.

"Through their profiles, Papa!" – Billy's son was genuinely surprised and also sounded a little irritable – "While you create your account, you also create your profile, which lists your mini resume, like your school, college, workplace, etc. Then Facebook automatically picks up common contacts from those institutes and suggests your friends. You won't know till you actually are in it. Interested?"

"Ummm… well let's give it a try" – said Billy, the picture of imaginary Molly still looming large in his mind.

In their desktop, Billy's son helped him first by opening a Gmail account, and then opened a Facebook profile attaching Dad's Gmail account. He also taught Billy the basics of Facebook. Billy was pleasantly surprised to discover Mrs. Brown there! He quickly sent a friend request to Mrs. Brown and his son. His son accepted it then and there through his smart phone. He also helped him to form a Family Group.

Billy was quick to learn the trick of finding friends, and he was delighted to discover that it was much easier than he thought.

And then to try, in the friend search box he typed 'Saumil Pandey'– his best friend in Engineering College. Facebook instantly listed more than ten Saumil Pandeys. But clearly he could detect the Saumil he was looking for, from the profile picture. Now he was bald, had put on considerable weight, yet was still distinctly distinguishable through his thick drooping moustache that had turned salt-pepper now. Happily, Billy sent a friend request.

He started ransacking his brain to recall names of his long lost friends… this wasn't a bad toy after all. In his next four attempts, he succeeded in finding two of his mates, one from school and the other from college. He immediately sent friends request to the two friends he just discovered.

Within half an hour, he got acceptance postings from the four requests he had sent a little earlier. He was thrilled. He saw a message pop-up from the bottom of his screen – Saumil had messaged him, live.

Thereafter he engaged in general chats with a couple of his long lost friends. It was good to catch up after so many years, but nothing great. Even while connected remotely, Billy could sense that all the characters had changed. They, for whatever reason, weren't the same persons that he knew in his school and college days. Most of his queries were answered with some kind of aloofness, covered in a frosty sheath. Their queries were also very matter-of-fact type. He started his chat with some expletives, which were part and parcel of their lingos when they were in college. He did not get similar reciprocation, which surprised Billy all ends up. The chats were more sort of formal. They lacked the warmth and informality for his liking.

Later in the night, Billy typed 'Molly Ray' in the friends search box, feeling a pang of guilt while doing so. At least three dozen Molly Rays sprang up, some with faces, some devoid of them. For Billy, it made little difference, for he'd never seen the real Molly, ever.

Yet he carefully went through the Mollys. Most of them were young looking and either students, or working somewhere. Then it struck Billy that Molly belonged to his same age group. And if she was working, she must've retired, like him. So he looked for a 'retired Molly'. There were none…

Tad disappointed he was wondering what to do next when it struck him that Molly Ray, post marriage, need not have retained the same surname. She can be a Sharma, Mishra, Gupta, Dutta, Ahluwalia…anything. If she got married that is.

This was turning out to be a bigger problem than he thought. He started thinking hard about some distinguishable feature to zero in on Molly, *his* Molly. Then he remembered, Molly studied in Howrah Girls High School. So this time he typed, 'Molly Howrah Girls School' in the search box. To his surprise, there were ten Mollys from Howrah Girls School. Some of them still students. And none from his age group.

Slowly it started to sink in his mind that Molly was lost forever from his life. For all he knew, she could have been dead long back.

***

Not being able to locate Molly Ray through Facebook, the very reason he'd opened his account, dwindled Billy's interest in Facebook rapidly. He started viewing Facebook as more of a self-advertising platform than anything else. It was a classic platform for narcissists, posting various photographs of themselves and their families, describing every minute details of what they do throughout the day. Eating out, travelling on business trips, travelling on pleasure trips, feeling happy, angry, sad – everything is posted with monotonous regularity. Soon Billy got bored with Facebook, big time.

He started receiving a few mails into his newly opened Gmail account from his friends. Even those failed to excite him. And then one day he received a mail from one Ms. Naina, with a subject line "Lonely Naina seeking your friendship".

Lonely Billy got interested in Lonely Naina. The moment he opened to mail, there were pop-ups, right, left and center on his desktop screen. One particular site – Lonelysingles.com – interested Billy. The site had pictures of skimpily clad females in provocative poses. Lonelysingles.com promised to end loneliness of lonely singles, once registered, by arranging suitable hook ups with other lonely souls in the planet, country, state and even the city…wow! Only Billy couldn't quite figure out why it required young skimpily dressed females to lure lonely singles…

He clicked on Lonelysingles.com. Instantly its home page opened, adorned with many more provocative females, and raunchy graphics! The flamboyance of the site made him a trifle nervous. He hadn't seen a site like that ever before in his rather short internet career! It also left him amused.

He located two tabs, one labeled as 'Sign In' and the other 'New User – Register'.

With unconscious spontaneity, Billy clicked on the New User button and started registering himself.

1. Option: Dropdown window gave many options, like, a man seeking a woman, a man seeking a man, a woman seeking a woman, a man seeking a couple etc. With trembling fingers Billy selected 'man seeking a woman'. Molly was a woman after all…
2. Name: That was easy. Billy typed his name with little more confidence than he had for filling Option Dropdown options.
3. Gender: Easier. But why was that necessary, thought Billy, once Option Dropdown was filled. It was obvious that he was a man.
4. Age: Billy filled up his birth date in the dd-mm-yyyy dropdown boxes. Once done, his age flashed as 62. This sounded unacceptable even to Billy. He revisited the dd-mm-yyyy drop down box and shaved off 27 years of his age. Now his age flashed at an acceptable 35.
5. Sexual orientation: Dropdown window gave three options, Billy chose 'Straight'.

….as Billy continued filling his profile, his confidence in this new-found game increased rapidly. He filled up the rest of the profile, which was more detailed than the longest CV he'd ever created, with tremendous alacrity. It went into the details of his income, social status, hobbies and even the kinkiness, if any, in his sexual desires (anal, threesomes, group sex, role-plays) as well as his own endowments…

Billy actually blushed as he filled in the details. Like his age, he also lied here and there. He increased his endowment by a good two inches, described himself as well built and fit, even chose his hair color as dark while all he had for hair on his skull were some sporadic grey growths which were also deserting him swiftly…

And then the portal asked for his photograph, which Billy promptly refused.

Pat flashed a warning message on the screen – "Chances of hook-ups increases if you post a photograph, you may reconsider your decision".

This made Billy think hard. What the portal said had some merit. Who would like to build relationship with a faceless entity? But uploading own picture was out of question. So he went to Google Image, selected an image of a reasonably handsome young male with Indian features and uploaded it…

Then, he e-sauntered into the site with some trepidation. Again pictures of lots of lonely singles invited him. It also showed a link on who's online. He clicked there. The profile shortlisted a few names with a green LED like glow by their sides, indicating that they were available, live.

Billy hesitated for a second, and then clicked on Sexysonam123 – who, if the portal information was to be believed, was within 3 km of his radius, live and itching.

Billy invited her for a private chat with a simple hi:

September 30, 2014, 2:33 pm

Hi

<Sorry Sexysonam123 did not accept your chat request>

Billy felt flabbergasted and even insulted to an extent. This was not in his equation. Why would Sexysonam123 reject his chat request without any rhyme or reason? She too was a lonely sole looking for partners, wasn't she? Embarrassed, he looked all around out of habit, only to realize that no one was watching him, for he was alone at home.

Billy's next choice was Charulekha_horny.

This time Billy chose to first go through the Lady's profile…

Hmmm … so Charulekha_horny was 37, divorced, had one grown up child, believed in one night stand, sex was always in her mind, looking for friends with benefits…

Friends with benefits! What exactly does that mean? Billy chose to explore. He pinged…

September 30, 2014, 2:40 pm

Hi

Billy waited for a whole minute with bated breath for something to happen. There were absolutely no movements from other end. And then as he was about to switch over to somebody else he saw on his screen:

<Charulekha_horny entered chat>

Hi

Hai

What do you do?

*F**k around, you?*

Billy never expected such a crass reply, that too, from a lady who was half his age. He felt his mouth turn dry. However, he was determined to carry on with the chat. He typed,

I work.

Ha ha … only work, no f**k ?

I am alone, so… Billy was at a loss for words

So u hlp urself wen ur horny? U ever get horny baby?

Mmmm … well …

Billy suddenly felt his heart was pumping harder. He wasn't used to such conversations.

Wats ur age?

35… Billy replied, remembering his profile age

Married?

Separated … you?

Billy lied again … picture of Mrs. Brown flashed in his mind while doing so.

Divorced silly. One kid. Dint u chk my prfle?

Well, not everything written in the profile is true, so I thought I'd ask.

Whr r u frm? Plc?

Mumbai. You?

Pune. Hey y dont u drv over to me????

Drive, to Pune?

Ys silly. Feeln lonly n horny. Whata u doin nw?

Chatting with you. You?

Don't f***ing act smart. Am lyin naked. Open your pants dude. Letz at least have some cybersex.

Cybersex! What are you talking about?

Don't f***ing behave asif you don't f***ing know. Wanna see my p***y? Chk out, jst sent you a pic...;). Send yours.

Billy Brown didn't know what to say. He could actually hear his heart beat like a jungle drum. For the first time he noticed an attachment along with the chat message. With trembling hands he clicked on the attachment. Almost immediately a picture of a stark naked woman with face covered and lying spread-eagled bloomed on his screen. Closing it in a hurry he instinctively looked around to check whether anybody noticed it, only to realize a nanosecond later that he was alone at home. With some effort he typed again...

Err...look can we chat decent

F*** Off...

<Charulekha_horny left the chat>

Billy felt flustered and hot under the collar. He'd never experienced anything like this ever. How could a 37 year old housewife behave in such undignified manner?

It took some time before he could come to terms to the female members of the lonelysingles.com site. He logged out of the site for a while, but soon his curiosity and loneliness got the better of him which forced him log into the site yet again ... and again... and again...

In the next few weeks, under the guise of a 35-year old virile and muscularly built single, he interacted with a wide range of weirdly named females each characteristically different from the other.

He came across one kalpana4u who claimed to be a 'docter' – probably the only doctor in the universe who did not know how to correctly spell her profession…

He chatted with sexy_sanjana who was only interested in risqué expletives in wrong English…

He interacted with hungry_kavitha who genuinely seemed to be a doctor, but was willing to sleep with him for some extra money which she needed desperately…

He ran into one shivani69 who was interested in meeting him only if he brought four other guys along – for she was only interested in group sex…

He encountered one Sangi-f**k who first wanted to know how much Billy could spend on her before she started her chat privately on skype…

He ran into poormadhu who claimed she was held captive by her husband and son – and wanted Billy to come in a shiny armor and rescue her …

He bumped into one natashasmith who had no pretensions about being a paid whore and was willing to spend the night at his place for a price …

He got frequent chat invitations from one gauri_sexy who enjoyed infidelity just for the heck of it …

He got in touch with a Bengali housewife - Droupadi – who, like the mythological character loved to simultaneously chat with four-five males, flaunting her vital statistics, describing her private parts with graphical accuracy…

Lascivious, lecherous, treacherous, libidinous, unfaithful, sadistic, perverted … in a matter of two weeks Billy Brown unlocked virtually all type of dark minds of the fairer sex which he, even in his wildest dreams, couldn't imagine to have existed…

There were very few who cared for decent companionship. It appeared to him as if the whole world was cluttered with itchy-bitchy sex maniacs…

He gradually got accustomed to the chat lingo and the use of occasional expletives. And he also got bored. One afternoon post lunch he was listlessly browsing through the site, when the profile of a new member caught his eye.

Kiara Rose. Age 23. Student. Not in a relationship. Bisexual. Hobbies: Poems and erotica!

The profile picture was that of a young girl with a well-developed body in the process of removing her jersey with her bra barely visible.

Interesting! Interesting name ... interesting profile ... interesting picture ...

Kiara Rose appeared vastly different from the numerous other profiles that he'd viewed in the past couple of weeks. He pinged her.

Hi

Billy waited with bated breath. Even though he was quite used to chatting now, somehow he badly wanted to chat with Kiara. After two or three seconds, Kiara pinged back

<Kiara Rose entered chat>

Hi

Wanna chat dirty or decent?

Depends on your mood. I'm game for both.

Hmmm...Kiara Rose...interesting name..

Not my real name, but I wish it was... I love the name... if i had the choice of selecting a name for myself again, it would be Kiara. Rose, coz i love roses (red roses to be specific)

You seem to be romantic type. Are u into reading and writing poems?

I love poems. Do you?

Billy was never into poems or literatures. For a moment he pondered on whether to tell the truth. But there was a risk. Ms. Rose might lose interest if he disclosed the truth, and dump him. Honestly, even in that short while, he found Kiara Rose refreshingly different. So he lied, again,

Yeah, of course. Who doesn't like poems? Don't get much time though.

And what do you do Mr. Brown?

I am a mining engineer. I work for a multinational company.

Not working today? Or r u chatting frm the office?

No, no, I'm home today. Wasn't keeping too well so decided to take a break. How about u?

Our college starts at 8:00 in the morning, and by two in the afternoon we are free. So r you married Mr. Brown?

I am. But now separated.

Oh, I'm sorry. Why, what went wrong? Mrs. Brown frigid in bed or something ? ;)

Hell, no, no… nothing like that …it's our mental differences, you know … the mental wavelength thing

Tch tch … too bad. And after how many years of marriage, Mr. Brown, may I ask.

*Ten … ten years …*Lies were coming out with relative ease now.

Any issues?

Yeah, one boy. Now 7 years.

Suggest you patch up with Mrs. Brown. Fighting parents have telling effect on kids.

Even though Billy had lied on everything that he said regarding his family, he was touched by the girl's sensitivity. He asked:

Tell me something about you. Are you in a relationship?

I was. But I just broke up.

That's awful. Why did you have to do that?

He doesn't want to be bound into any kind of commitments. Whenever I talk of our future, he kind of avoids. After trying for five years I decided to dump him last month. It's very painful, Mr. Brown. I still can't get him out of my mind.

Look Kiara, it seems u still hv a soft corner for the guy. Try and patch up. May be he's got other priorities now. May be he's got some responsibilities which is forcing him into behaving the way he's doing.

I'll take a note of your advice. But as of now, I want to concentrate only on my career, and nothing else. I'm doing my MBA on HR and Finance.

Wow. Kiara, now you r giving me a complex. I could never manage an admission in MBA, even though the competition, then, was far lesser.

And when was that, Mr Brown, you sound as if you belong to pre-historic age…

Billy quickly calculated. His portal age now is 35, so he should've done his graduation 13 years back. *12- 13 years before …*

That's not too long ago …

Is that you, Kiara, I mean the provocative lady in the profile picture?

Of course not, do you think I'm a fool? And Kiara is not my real name either. I am Rhea. Rhea Roy.

Rhea … very modern name … Roy — are you a Bengali? I have a Bengali friend who's a Roy.

I'm half Bengali. My mother is a Bengali. I have my roots in Calcutta but born and brought up in Hyderabad. And you? Is Billy Brown your real name?

Well, of course. What made you think it wasn't? By the way, aren't you scared to disclose so much personal details to a stranger like me?

You are a good person, I know that. You won't cause any harm to me.

And may I ask how do you know that?

My intuitions. I'm usually right. Only Nikhil was a mistake.

Nikhil?

My bloke with whom I broke up recently. But I'm sure you won't be like Nikhil.

Hey hang on. You are not eyeing me as a replacement for your Nikhil, are you?

Lol. What's wrong in that Mr. Brown?
As such you are not getting along with
your wifey. I'm a decent girl.

Billy was dumbstruck. He was way too older than Rhea, and happily married.
The girl must be joking.

How's that possible?

Why not? Well where are you from?

I too had my roots in Bengal, a long,
long time ago. Now settled in Mumbai.

Mumbai … Wow. City of my dreams.
Been there twice. I too would like to
settle there. One more reason for me to
go after you Mr. Brown. Lol.

That's…that's preposterous. I'm not
looking for any relationship. Not again.
Billy thought it was cheeky of him to
play the strained-relationship card on
which he'd earlier lied.

Ha ha – I can see somebody's nervous.
Don't worry Mr. Brown. I'm not gonna
jump on your shoulders … not yet.
Perhaps, we should share our phone
numbers, email ids and pictures first.
What do you say?

Email id is fine. It's too early to share
phone numbers and pictures.

Lol. You are more scared than a girl
Mr. Brown. C'mon don't be a sissy.
Rhea_Roy91@yahoo.co.in – that's my
email id. What's yours?

It's Billybrown12345@gmail.com. Keep
mailing me. Honestly I do not quite
enjoy logging into this site anymore.

Sure, Mr. Brown. I agree. Most males in this site are substandard sex maniacs. Not my type. Shall hookup through mails. Gotta go now. Bye.

<Kiara Rose left chat>

Billy Brown logged out of the site and sat quietly for a while, trying to ponder over the chat he'd just had with Rhea Roy alias Kiara Rose in the past half an hour. This girl was definitely different from the other ones that he'd met so far. She loved poems and erotica – what a diversified combination! A half-Bengali – had roots in Calcutta but born and brought up in Hyderabad. She'd just dumped her boyfriend of five years because he was non-committal. What was she up to? Was she contemplating a relationship with Billy, or was she just pulling his legs?

He googled for the meaning of Kiara. It was derived from Ciaran which in Gaelic meant little dark one. Ciara or Kiara was the female form. As per the Urban Dictionary Kiara meant a beautiful girl, always nice and funny who will always cheer you up when you are sad. Also a great person to be around, just someone you have to love.

Thereafter, regular chatting with Rhea Roy became a routine. Almost every afternoon, after lunch, Billy Brown logged into the lonelysingles.com site and waited for Rhea to join. He pretended to do it from his workstation at his office. If for some reason, she failed to turn up, Billy pinged some other females. But he could find nobody else who could match Rhea in intellect and wit. In course of their chats, they explored and discovered each other. Rhea explained in great details on her projects, her poems, her classmates, teachers and her ex-boyfriend – Nikhil. Billy on the other hand narrated his experiences in Mining, his hostel life, funny incidents involving his friends and mostly about his separated wife and his current state of loneliness. All his stories related to his married life were false, of course, aimed to invoke sympathy from Rhea.

Every chat session, drew Rhea closer to Billy, bit by bit, even without her realizing it. The chat sessions also started bordering around subtle eroticism. One day Rhea even disclosed her physical relationship with Nikhil, at times a bit too explicitly for Billy's comfort. And then she started asking pointed questions on his sex life, which Billy either avoided or lied.

Lonelysingles.com site was also growing in popularity. Every day there were more and more new members swarming in, which made the site slower and slower. Sometimes it took more than a minute for a chat message to reach. Finally, one day they decided to hookup mostly through emails.

Inevitably, the chat sessions left Billy cheerful and buoyant. However, his mirth lasted only till the time when Mrs. Brown got back from work. These days, Mrs. Brown was always in a cross mood after the day's work. A demanding boss, Mumbai traffic and the menopause which she'd recently attained all contributed to her irritation – thought Billy.

She also had to do all household chores. Billy had never cooked. His knowledge of cooking was limited to boiling eggs and – after the tea bags appeared in the market – brewing tea. This he did by boiling water in an electric kettle, for Mrs. Brown would never allow him to turn on the gas stove. Also, Mrs. Brown was quite fussy on operating the washing machine – she'd never allow him to handle that. She was sure that if she allowed him do some household work, he would cause more damage than help. For example if Billy operated the washing machine, he would definitely mix the colored clothes with the white ones, he would definitely not add the right quantity of washing powder, he would not set the soak-timing properly. She was also obsessed with cleanliness. Everyday all floors had to be swept and mopped. All furniture had to be dusted. All upholstery vacuumed. If any day the household help – an elderly Maharastrian maid – failed to report for work, Mrs. Brown turned hysterical. And such days were not infrequent. Unannounced absenteeism was one trait which was religiously followed by all house-maids irrespective of their caste, creed or religion in Indian cities. However, that did not deter Mrs. Brown to slacken her obsession towards maintaining cleanliness. If the maid did not turn up, she herself would take up the broom and mop and clean the floors – which, Billy thought, was totally unnecessary. This added to her pressures and ultimately her health and ill temper.

That morning the maid had bunked. After dinner, Mrs. Brown quickly cleaned up the table and retired early. Sex had long gone into hibernation from the Browns' bedroom. Neither of them felt any urge to make love any more. Their conversations were limited only to general household discussions, nothing beyond.

Billy Brown looked at his wife's sleeping countenance and felt a pang of guilt. Was he cheating on his wife? – He questioned himself. He wasn't sure whether chatting with unknown females over the net with a disguised identity and lying right, left and center on his marital status also amounted to cheating or not. Much as he tried to keep the guilt out of his mind, it kept coming back. Strangely, he felt a strong urge to go back to the computer and surf all the same.

Mrs. Brown was fast asleep which was evident from the soft snoring sound. Billy tip-toed out of the bedroom and sat on his desktop. He quickly logged into his email account and was delighted to discover a mail – from Rhea Roy.

The mail was sent at 6:35 pm.

He clicked on the mail.

From: Rhea Roy <u>Rhea_Roy91@yahoo.co.in</u>
To: Billy Brown <u>Billybrown12345@gmail.com</u>
Sent: Friday, 24 April, 6:35 pm
Sub: A distant star twinkling in the night sky

Dear Mr. Brown,

Chatting with you was really rejuvenating. It seems at last I have found someone who shares common interests with me. Something tells me that you can be trusted. I am more than happy to have you in my contacts. Hoping we will stay in touch and not carelessly lose each other's company.....

Well, i love reading thriller, romantic and erotic novels, writing poems and listening to music depending on my mood.

Allow me to share my latest poem ...

And then she went on with a poem on a distant star in a chilly night, yet providing the warmth for she related the star to her long lost love whatever whatever...

Billy read and re-read the poem three-four times, but failed to comprehend it fully. However, the text seemed to be good, and so the choice of words. The girl had determinedly concluded that Billy was into poems and all.

This left Billy in a spot of bother. He was hell bent to impress Rhea. He must think of a suitable reply. Best would be to reply with a poem. But Billy knew, it would take more than a lifetime for him to churn out a few lines. Mrs. Brown liked poems. Suddenly he remembered she'd shared a poem with him and his son a few days back. He didn't read it though. Suddenly, with all the urgency of the world, he flicked through his mobile for the old whatsapp message from his wife. Huh – there it was. This was written by one Mary Elizabeth Frye. He read that twice and thought it was quite okay. In fact after the third reading, he found it good, and after the fourth, he thought it was great!

He hit the reply button in Rhea's mail and typed, laboriously:

From: Billy Brown <Billybrown12345@gmail.com>
To: Rhea Roy <Rhea_Roy91@yahoo.co.in>
Sent: Friday, 24 April, 11.05 pm
Sub: Re: A distant star twinkling in the night sky

Dear Rhea,

You wrote that? OMG (His numerous chat sessions had already made him chat-abbreviation savvy) ... *this is unbelievable. You are one hell of a talented young lady. I'm sure you are one of those topper types. I did not understand what you meant by "carelessly lose each other's company..." Wish you could've been little more specific honey. But then, deciphering girls had been an age old mystery...and will continue to be so...*

Since you like poems, here is one poem which I particularly like. No it's not written by me ... I'm not half as talented as you. This was penned by the famous Ms. Mary Elizabeth Frye (Billy wasn't sure whether Ms. Frye was indeed so famous or not, but what the hell! And if Mrs. Brown liked it, it must be good! He went on to type out the poem in the whatsapp message sent by his wife, word by word)

Do not stand at my grave and weep
I am not there. I do not sleep.
I am a thousand winds that blow.
I am the diamond glints on snow.
I am the sunlight on ripened grain.
I am the gentle autumn rain.
When you awaken in the morning's hush
I am the swift uplifting rush
Of quiet birds in circled flight.
I am the soft stars that shine at night.

Do not stand at my grave and cry;
I am not there. I did not die.

Dunno why, these days i feel very bereft of everything. Probably that's the reason i like the above poem ... where the poet shows hope even in bereavement!

You mentioned you loved erotica. How can somebody who is so deeply in love with poetry and literature also indulge in pornography? Do you write erotic stories also?

You wished me a happy weekend, but let me tell you, nowadays I hate weekends. It only compounds my melancholy. On weekdays, at least I am busy with my work. While the world rejoices in weekend, I weep within myself. I long for the Monday to arrive. Anyway ...screw the self-pity. Now that you have come into my life, it ain't gonna be so lonely I guess...

Billy paused. He re-read the last line and found it a little too explicit. He rephrased it as:

Now that I have you as my friend, life on weekends will not be so boring and lonely I guess...

Well, it's quite late now. I hope you are peacefully asleep, dreaming about your loved ones.

Best Regards,

Billy Brown.

Billy logged out and went to bed. Mrs. Brown was sleeping like a baby, curled up in a fetal pose and clutching a pillow. She looked peaceful and contented. He looked at the woman who'd been his wife for the past 33 years. When they were married, she was only 23 years – just about Rhea's age. She was quite attractive with her round face and a mop of curly locks that gave her a doll like appearance. She had a permanent glowing tan, and rather long limbs – a rarity amongst Indian girls. She had been a devoted wife and an excellent mother. Till today, for her, the family was everything. Her biggest entertainments were family dinner and family outing. Their son was now independent and lived in Pune. Yet she would rather wait for him to get back on weekends and go for a family dinner together at some restaurant, than go only with her husband alone.

Billy felt the guilt pricking again. He lied down beside his wife and slept fitfully.

Billy waited for the weekend to pass, so that he could once again be home alone and resume his chat and email sessions.

On Monday, after Mrs. Brown left for work, the first thing he did was to switch on the desktop and log into his email.

He expected mails from Rhea and he wasn't disappointed. The mail in his inbox was having a few attachments.

From: Rhea Roy <Rhea_Roy91@yahoo.co.in>
To: Billy Brown <Billybrown12345@gmail.com>
Sent: Saturday, 25 April, 2:35 pm
Sub: Planning a new erotica.

Dear Mr. Brown,

Thanks for sharing Madame Frye's poem. I absolutely loved it. It shows that I was right in assessing you as a person. You are a sensitive, caring and romantic individual – my type. I think our wavelengths have matched, and we shall rock together. And you are handsome too. So what if you are a tad older? I'd love to have you as my friend, forever.

I feel blessed to have a friend like you and would like to have you as a friend who would never break my trust, that's what I meant by "carelessly lose each other's company". And I know you won't.

And what exactly do you mean by 'deciphering girls' Mr. Brown? Sorry to say, but your choice of words are inappropriate when it comes to judging the female psychology, because, there's really nothing to decipher. Let me tell you women have brain cells that help them in thinking and doing multiple things at a time, whereas the men have single celled brains that enable them think only one thing at a time. Women are natural with their multi-tasking abilities, whereas men have single track mind, and that's why men find women mysterious and complex.

Oh, yes I love erotica, but not those 'Mast-Ram' types that are available at the country street-sides. Erotica does not necessarily mean pornography. D.H.Lawrence's "Lady Chatterly's Lover" was once an erotica, is now regarded as a classic. Same is true for Vladimir Nobokov's "Lolita". Have you read them? I would also recommend Irving Wallace's "The Seven Minutes" – which would clear your misconception about erotica.

Amongst the modern day authors – have you read E.L.James? I recommend you read "The Fifty Shades of Grey" by Ms James. It's available online. It's the first of the Grey trilogy and it's amazing! I am submissively in love with the protagonist hero – Christian Grey. I've read it many times. Every time I did, I imagined myself to be Anastasia Steele whom Mr. Grey loved, enslaved, dominated and playfully persecuted. Domination in bed turns me on. How about you, Mr. Brown? Who'd been the dominating partner in bed, you or Mrs. Brown?

By the way, after I started communicating with you I'm feeling a bit naughty. And whenever I feel naughty, I resort to erotica. I am planning to write an erotica with you as a protagonist. Would you mind, Mr. Brown? Would you be my Christian Grey in real life?

Hope you are having an exciting weekend. I know you are alone, so go out – eat, drink and make merry. Make life exciting. Hey, why don't you fly over to Hyderabad one weekend, Mr. Brown?

Let me now tell you, like you, my parents are separated and divorced. I live with my Dad. My Sunday's are reserved for my Dad. No laptops, no work, no studies, no messaging, no nothing.

I am attaching three pictures of mine. The first one is a selfie solo pic. The second one was at a resort which we visited along with some of my college friends, and the last one is with Nikhil – my ex, on the day I'd graduated.

Love and hugs (in a friendly way)

Rhea.

Billy clicked on the first attachment. A picture of a young and rather attractive damsel wearing a crimson sleeveless evening gown blossomed on his screen. Her skin was a light brown and eyes were so dark that they glittered like polished onyx, surrounded by thick lashes. She was slightly overweight that could be managed with diet and exercise. She had thick black straight hair flowing copiously over her rather broad shoulders. She had a soft stomach – which had a tendency to bulge out with age if she wasn't careful, and large breasts. Her white pearl necklace – quite in contrast to her skin and her crimson dress – nestled carelessly over her ample breasts only helped in pronouncing the cleavage. Rather provocative – thought Billy.

He opened the second picture – she was easily distinguishable in a group of girls and boys in a fun-park – in her jeans and red tees.

In the third picture she was wearing the black graduation robe and the cap and she had a somber looking well-built young man with sleepy eyes by her side. So that was Nikhil – Rhea's ex.

After re-reading the mail Billy had an uncomfortable feeling. Was this girl falling for him? Is she building a castle of dreams around the muscular and handsome man whose picture he'd used as the profile photo? The handsome lonely soul, engineer, reasonably well to do, who shared common interests?

Oh my God, Billy realized that he was cheating not one but two women simultaneously. Some achievement for a retired 62 year old!

But he was not ready to give up – not yet. This Rhea episode was like a fresh whiff of air in his otherwise sedate and boring life. He could feel a fresh flow of testosterone through his system, causing his heart to pump more rapidly than usual. Billy was on a hypertension drug since long. He was sure that in spite of having his daily doses, his BP had gone up by a few notches after this Rhea episode. But what the hell! As Rhea said in her mail – what's life without a little excitement?

He went to Google and typed 'Fifty Shades of Grey online'…

For the next two hours, Billy glimpsed through the pdf version of E.L.James' 'Fifty Shades of Grey'. He found it abhorring. This was not the first time Billy was exposed to pornography – he'd read them during his college days for their hostels were flooded with pornographic stuff. Graphical description of lovemaking between a man and woman – irrespective of the relations they share – as long as it is plain and straight can be made digestible. But what he found in Ms. James' book was utterly distasteful. It was all about domination of an obnoxiously rich man over a woman – Anastasia Steele – in bed, whom she actually binds through a contract. A contract for bondage, blinding and fucking! And the woman was actually willfully accepting and enjoying it! Which modern day female would allow such submission just for the sake of sex? Would she have enjoyed if Christian Grey was not super rich living in super luxury condos and flying in private aircrafts, but a common man with ordinary looks but better loving capabilities? Billy opted out of the site after reading about one third of the book for he could not sustain any more of that.

Billy was getting more and more convinced that Rhea and he were more different than chalk and cheese.

He logged into his email, and clicked the reply button to Rhea's latest mail.

From: Billy Brown <Billybrown12345@gmail.com>
To: Rhea Roy <Rhea_Roy91@yahoo.co.in>
Sent: Monday, 27 April, 13:13 pm
Sub: Re: Planning a new erotica

Dear Ms. Rose,

Hope you had a grand Sunday with your Daddy. Didn't know your parents were divorced. Sorry about that.

Weekends for me are boring. This time it was no exception. I did nothing. Just lazed around and hoped it passed quickly. No, I did not venture out and seek excitement per your advice. I am very choosy about my companions. I just cannot socialize with anybody and everybody. With you around, it could have been different though. But geographically I think we are a thousand kilometers apart.

Boy, you are quite a dish! I hope you won't mind my saying that. I kept ogling at your selfie for hours together. That Nikhil chap must be a fool, to let go of a girl like you so easily. You are one of the rare combinations of beauty and brains. However, may I ask you what made you share your pictures with me? You don't even know me properly. A word of caution, Ms. Rose – please don't trust strangers so easily and post your pictures to all and sundry. In this digital age, the pictures can be mal-utilized big time.

I haven't read all those books you'd recommended, but I did go through 'Fifty Shades of Grey'. Honestly I didn't find it very interesting. Rather, at times, I found it disgusting. My idea of loving is way apart from those kinky stuffs the author made her protagonists do. And worst of all, Anastasia was enjoying it. I do not see how a girl like you having logical opinions and feministic sparks idolizes a dud like Christian Grey. I found him dark.

Sorry, I have no intentions of becoming your Mr. Grey.

Mr. Brown respects Ladies. He likes to handle them with utmost care and not use them like doormats like many do. He likes to love and be loved, but he also likes to keep a sharp divide between pleasure and pain.

By all means use me as your protagonist in your erotica. But do not make me perform those masochistic activities like your revered Mr. Christian Grey.

Love (friendly)
William Brown.

From: Rhea Roy <Rhea_Roy91@yahoo.co.in>
To: Billy Brown <Billybrown12345@gmail.com>
Sent: Monday, 27 April, 6:45 pm
Sub: Re Re Planning a new erotica.

Dear Mister William Brown,
Why did you have to address me as Ms. Rose when you knew my real name? Do you find Kiara Rose sexier?

Please stop worrying about my pictures Billy boy. I know you are a harmless man and will not misuse my pics. I also know whom to post and whom not to. Stop playing the role of big Daddy. I would rather imagine you as my lover!

I must say you have no idea, Mr. Brown, on the sexual behaviors and desires of a woman. As a matter of fact, assertive and dominant women prefer to hand over the reins in the bed and enjoy dominations. But the reverse is not always true. Socially dominant women – the typical type-A females - enjoy sexual submission fantasies more than other women. So what you considered as persecution in bed, may actually turn out to be more pleasurable ;). Say what Mr. Brown, come out of your gentle garb and try out a little masochism – next time you make love to your wife – if you make love to your wife that is… Mrs. Brown may actually love it.

If I ever meet you, Billy, I'm gonna eat you. I'm gonna teach you all the arts and sciences of treating a female. You found Christian Grey dark. But remember, Brown is a darker shade than Grey. I will see to it that Mr. William Brown turns out darker than Mr. Christian Grey in bed.

However, as of now, I shall respect your wish. I have started writing the much awaited erotica. You are my hero, but relax – I shall not taint your character by forcing masochism on him. Not yet. I shall reserve it for some time in future, when I convince you about controlled sadism in bed. Billy Brown – I'm quite fascinated by the name. So I chose to retain your real name; hope will not have any objections to that. Besides, there are thousands of William Browns around the world.

I've written 20 pages in two hours and still have more to add to it!!! Writing after a long time so I just hope it turns out as good as you are expecting it to be.

Feeling it as I'm thinking about you and writing it. Omg, Mr. Brown, you are turning me into a horny li'l bitch as I write…

Hugs and kisses,
Yours
Kiara Rose.

Billy went through the mail three-four times, and then sat like a zombie. He could sense that this girl was completely mesmerized by the virtual Billy Brown – which was a far cry from his real self. Worse still, she was trying to discover her Christian Grey through him! Something, he sensed, was not right.

The next day, after Mrs. Brown left for work, Billy Brown found the next mail from Rhea Roy sitting quietly in his mailbox. The mail had a pdf attachment.

He opened the mail.

From: Rhea Roy <Rhea_Roy91@yahoo.co.in>
To: Billy Brown <Billybrown12345@gmail.com>
Sent: Tuesday, 28 April, 2:14 am
Sub: My new erotica – enjoy

Dear Billy,

Enclosing my new erotica. Hope you find this … err … stirring.

I am not ashamed to admit that writing this made me very, very excited, and my longing for you has increased manifold. I am in a continuous state of stimulation …and I am happy…

I must thank you Mr. Brown for helping me to come out of the depression after I threw Nikhil out of my life. The incident had left me scarred and listless which started affecting my studies. I had been a topper all through my career, but after Nikhil left, my grades started falling. I had lost all interest in completing my projects, and it started reflecting on my performance. Then suddenly you came in my life.

It doesn't matter, Mr. Brown, if you are married or not. It doesn't matter even if you are older than what your profile says. It also doesn't matter if that bloke in the picture is not the real you. What matters most is that in you I have found a true friend who understands me. I have found a shoulder which I can lean upon when I'm down and out. I know, whenever I'm in distress, you will always be there with your helping hand. You are a person I can trust my life with. Am I wrong in my assessment Billy? Don't tell me yes, for that will break my heart.

Also, I honestly want you to go back to Mrs. Brown – at least for the sake of your boy. Nobody knows better than I how it feels when parents are separated. I had gone through it myself. I really don't care if you patch up with your wife – only I request you to be available for me as well, whenever I need you. Be there as my friend, guide and yes, my lover. I do not know whether you still have any soft corner for your wife, but I really don't care even if you have. All I want from you is attention – no matter even if it is a divided attention.

Let me tell you now, my Mom has remarried and is settled in Mumbai. I'd visited her before. I have an open invitation from her to visit Mumbai anytime I wish to. I intend to come down to Mumbai after my exams – won't you meet me then, Mr. William Brown? The geographical distance that you'd mentioned will be surmounted, and we can have a rocking time together.

For now – enjoy my new story – "The Champagne"

Love and kisses,
Only yours,
Rhea.

Billy sighed and click-opened the pdf attachment.

The story titled "The Champagne". Billy read the story with unabated breath. It was simply unputdownable. Words flowed with mellifluous fluidity. The buildup was titillating and suspenseful, and the climax was uninhibited. The structure of the story followed the same pattern as in their cyber-friendship...

The female protagonist – Kiara Rose – was a working lady, single, talented and provocative. She gets acquainted with William Brown through a social networking site. Interestingly, unlike the virtual William who was only 35, the William in her story was much older – above 50 – who had a history of heart attack, and a disrupted marriage. Much in the same pattern as Billy had described through the various sessions of chats. One evening, after a hard day's work, Kiara engages herself with a chat session with William, enjoying a glass of French champagne which she'd acquired during her last business trip to Paris. In course of the chat, she drinks a glass too many, until the champagne gets the better of her. Their chats turn erotic, and at one point of time she suggests they talk over phone, instead. William calls up only to discover a provocative and husky voice waiting hungrily at the other end. The gradually start talking dirty and end up having a violent session of phone sex – all the while, Kiara taking the role of dominant partner and ordering William his moves...

When they are done, they mull over the beautiful feeling they'd just experienced. Kiara promises to get back again on Friday evening with another glass of champagne. She orders William to be available and charged up for the next session …She had a limitless stock of champagne…The story ends there.

Content wise, Billy found this to be better than "The Fifty Shades…" and definitely more erotic. Rhea Roy was affirmatively talented.

However, Billy was not elated. Much as he liked the attachment, he did not like the tone of the mail. The girl was slowly but steadily falling for him – more as a refuge or a substitution in the virtual world till she gets her next beau in the real world. She really did not bother about Billy's age. What made her age William beyond 50 in her tale? Billy always maintained he was only 35. Was this some kind of uncanny hunch that females have? She was looking for a relationship, and that clearly was not acceptable. She was ready even if Billy continued with dual relationships – both with her and his wife! And worst of all, she had a connection in Mumbai. Her own Mom lived here.

He started this as a pastime game – to relieve himself from his ennui in the long lonely afternoons. But he never expected such turn of events. He decided to play low key and refrained from replying immediately. He simply logged out and switched off his desk-top.

That evening Mrs. Brown returned from work with a high fever. She was barely able to walk. Somehow she entered the apartment and flopped on her bed. Billy was concerned, but Mrs. Brown was more concerned about how the household will run with her being bedridden. What would Billy eat for dinner? Who would do the dishes? Would Billy be able to do the laundry? There were no vegetables or fish in the fridge, who's going to stock it up – and without the fridge stocked up Billy will have to live on dal-rice? What will their son eat when he visits them over the weekend? Even while sick, all Mrs. Brown could think of was only of Billy and their son…

Billy called on the doctor, who diagnosed it as a viral attack. He prescribed paracetamols and vitamins, and advised increased fluid intake. The fever should not be allowed to shoot up, so he advised head-baths with normal tap water and application of wet sponge on her forehead from time to time. If the fever did not ebb in next 3 days – he advised a few tests to rule out infection.

Billy felt very sorry for the wife. He was not used to see Mrs. Brown sick – for she never was sick. He looked at his wife, now lying straight on her bed, her face rubicund with the heat. She was in a semi-conscious state, yet mumbling utterings like "Tonight you will have to manage with dal-rice … there's some left over in the fridge … also there's milk and cornflakes … you like cornflakes and cold milk, don't you …stop worrying … I'll be okay tomorrow…"

His old guilt weighed heavy on him. He felt, he was responsible for his wife's sickness. This somehow was a consequence of his sins for cheating on his devoted wife. He pleaded his wife to keep quiet and try to sleep…

Throughout the night Billy sat beside his wife, sponging her forehead, monitoring her temperature every couple of hours and administering paracetamol every four hours. She slept fitfully, occasionally waking up and reprimanding Billy for not sleeping.

Towards the dawn, only after the fever ebbed, did Billy fall sleep for a while.

Mrs. Brown, however, was in bed rest for the next four days. Much to the chagrin of his wife, Billy did not allow her to get up even for the smallest of reasons. For the first time in his life he managed to cook *khichri* for their meals after taking step-by-step instructions from the wife. He also did the laundry, dried and folded the washed clothes, got them pressed through the local press-*wallah*, and even bought fish, veggies and fruits before their son visited them on Friday evening. Luckily, the house maid did not bunk – so he did not have to sweep or mop.

Mrs. Brown, still weak from the violent viral fever, managed to shrug off the initial concern on how her husband will manage household chores while she was ill and slowly started enjoying the grind that Billy was going through.

On Friday she managed to walk around the apartment but Billy forced her away from any household work. At bedtime, Mrs. Brown drew herself closer to Billy and said,

"It's good I fell ill."

"Why do you say that? I was so worried."

"There's a good side of everything. The last four days made you grow-up"

"I always maintained I could manage the household chores. Only you never allowed me. You always thought I'd damage everything. I am not a kid" – Billy grunted.

Mrs. Brown drew more closer, rested her chin on Billy's chest and said,

"Oh you are. A big kid! But now the kid is growing up. All these days I kept worrying on what will happen to you if ever something happens to me; now I know you can manage, I can die in peace."

"Don't ever say that" – said Billy, clasping his palm over her lips – "I'll be finished without you. Chronologically, I am supposed to go before you. I'd prefer it that way."

"Shut up" – said Mrs. Brown and planted a kiss on Billy's lips.

They kissed after, what it seemed like, eons!

***

Next Monday, after Mrs. Brown left for work, Billy opened his mail-box. There was a flurry of mails from Rhea Roy waiting for him. He opened them chronologically.

From: Rhea Roy <Rhea_Roy91@yahoo.co.in>
To: Billy Brown <Billybrown12345@gmail.com>
Sent: Tuesday, 28 April, 10:17 pm
Sub: Fw: My new erotica – enjoy

Dear Billy-boy,

I was grossly disappointed to find no mail from you in my inbox. Did you go through "The Champagne?" I expected a mail with your comments, however, I am willing to give you benefit of doubt. You must've had a busy day and didn't get time to open your mailbox. I'm dying to get your feedback.

I value your comments – you mean so much to me now.

Hugs and kisses
Rhea.

***

From: Rhea Roy <Rhea_Roy91@yahoo.co.in>
To: Billy Brown <Billybrown12345@gmail.com>
Sent: Wednesday, 29 April, 3:35 pm
Sub: Fw Fw My new erotica – enjoy

Dear Mr. Brown,

It seems you still did not get time to read my piece. The boss has overloaded you with work or what? Say what – chuck the job and look for some other opportunities. You deserve better. Ever since I wrote the story, you are always on my mind. And there's one more thing with which my mind is occupied 24x7. Sex. I badly want to get laid.

> Erotically yours,
> Ms. Rose.

***

From: Rhea Roy <*Rhea_Roy91@yahoo.co.in*>
To: Billy Brown <*Billybrown12345@gmail.com*>
Sent: Thursday, 30 April, 1:15 am
Sub: This is mean…

Mr. Brown,

This is very mean of you. Here I am dying to hear from you, and there you have completely eradicated Ms. Rose from your mind. You don't seem to care for anything or anybody, do you? You are too f***ing engrossed with your own self. Why would you care if a poor li'l girl spent sleepless nights in Hyderabad?

Are you upset with me Mr. Brown, for using your character in my erotica? I know you are a purist by nature, one of your many traits that I admire. If you are, I promise not to use you ever in any of my stories. I will also change the name of my male protagonist in "The Champagne" if you so wish. But please reply.

> Yours,
> Kiara.

***

From: Rhea Roy <*Rhea_Roy91@yahoo.co.in*>
To: Billy Brown <*Billybrown12345@gmail.com*>
Sent: Friday, 1 May, 2:14 am
Sub: IS EVERYTHING OK?

Dear Billy,

Is everything okay? I have a feeling something's wrong somewhere. How's your health? Oh hell, why the f**k haven't I kept your cell number? Mine is 8227950509. If you see this mail, can you give me a call, please? I am worried stiff. You stay alone, do you need help? Omg how'm I gonna help you from here? I also tried the Lonelysingles.com site to look for you, but you weren't there either.

Do you have good neighbors who can help you when you are indisposed? I pray to God so that everything's okay.

Love
Rhea.

***

From: Rhea Roy <Rhea_Roy91@yahoo.co.in>
To: Billy Brown <Billybrown12345@gmail.com>
Sent: Saturday, 2 May, 11:11 pm
Sub: I am coming to Mumbai

Mr. Brown,

Are you avoiding me or has something happened to you? I am very worried.

This afternoon I spoke to my Mom. I told you earlier – she's remarried and settled in Worli, Mumbai. I talked to her about you. I told her that you are an old friend – nothing more. Should you need any help – and I'm sure you need - please call her. She's Mrs. Molly Khandelkar – 9820179796.

Next Friday is a holiday. I plan to use the extended weekend to travel to Mumbai. You mentioned in one of your early chat sessions you lived in Goregaon East, in a locality called Gokuldham. I would definitely see you there.

Please reply Billy – I am unable to concentrate on anything till I hear from you.

Lovingly yours,
Rhea.

***

Billy was stupefied!

The least that he expected was Rhea visiting Mumbai. Her mother – now re-married – Mrs Molly Khandelkar lives in Worli. Long, long ago there was a Molly in his life. Molly Ray – his pen-friend in school.

The deceitful game that he'd now got involved into also started with his quest for the long-lost pen-friend, Molly.

To break his ennui, he'd surfed for Molly – only to end up in enrolling in a sex-site and get entangled with one Rhea Roy – alias Kiara Rose…

Rhea … Rhea Roy! Molly Ray!

Billy knew, Ray and Roy is a common Bengali surname – which essentially was one and the same. Ray was often spelt as Roy and vice-versa.

Is it possible that Rhea was the daughter of Molly Ray – *his* Molly from his schooldays?

A long-shot;but possible. Or was it just a coincidence? He could easily find that out now. Solution to the mystery was just a phone call away…

Rhea had indeed mentioned once that she was half-Bengali and had her roots in Calcutta!

Strangely, Billy never felt the urge to call up Mrs. Molly Khandelkar and enquire. Even if Mrs. Khandelkar happened to be his long lost pen-friend Molly Ray, they had travelled huge distances along divergent paths in their lives. Trying to converge it would only create complications which both of them will find hot to handle. Best would be to bury the past in the sands of time…

Billy sat like a statue for a while, trying to assess his next move. There was no doubt that Rhea Roy had madly fallen for him. It was evident from her mails which reflected her possessiveness and her genuine worry for him. But why – wondered Billy. Was it because of the name? Was it because of his profile? A lonely well-to-do engineer, separated, having own car and place in Mumbai looking for companionship – sounded romantic. Or was it because of the present mental state of Rhea – after the break-up with her boyfriend?

He mulled over his next move for a while before energizing his computer, which had gone on a sleep mode, to send out a reply – which he knew was going to be the last mail from Billy Brown to Rhea Roy …

From: Billy Brown <Billybrown12345@gmail.com>
To: Rhea Roy <Rhea_Roy91@yahoo.co.in>
Sent: Monday, 4 May, 3:30 pm
Sub: Dear Rhea…

Dear Rhea,

Just went through all your mails. Please do not be perturbed, I'd been fine; hale and hearty as ever.

First let me compliment you on the excellent story. You are a talented young lady and a natural writer…In fact I rate you better than your E.L.James!

I found you refreshingly different right from the time we first chatted in that weird sex site. We clicked as friends, and honestly, I wanted to keep it that way. But from your last few mails, I noticed the friendship level from your side has taken a new turn. You are getting mentally involved with me, which I think is improper.

I think the real reason behind this is your break up with Nikhil. There is no doubt you still love him. He gets a mention in all your correspondences. You even shared his photo with me. Quite a good looking young man, I should say. Much more handsome than me, I must admit. Let me tell you here, the guy you see in my profile picture is not me. I am not that good looking – just average. Besides, I am much older, married, and have many responsibilities. Not a very bankable option for you, I daresay. On the other hand – look at Nikhil. You know him for the past five years. He's just about your age, perhaps a tad older. I am sure he is yet to be settled in his life, and that, in all probability, is the reason behind his remaining non-committal. But remember, despite that, he stuck with you. It's you who dumped him, right?

Let me share a secret with you here. Indian men, in general – strong as they appear from outside – are really weak mentally. Practically all men from the middle and even upper middle class think five times before willfully taking any responsibility. Almost all of them would first like to settle in life and then get married. I too was no different. I started working when I was twenty three – but got married only when I was twenty nine – that too after a lot of persuasion from my Mom. I suppose this is the exact reason behind Nikhil's apathy towards a commitment. Suggest, you give him some more time.

And if it still doesn't work out, give a damn. You are beautiful, young, educated, intelligent and talented. You are also confident. So why worry? Concentrate on building a career – and you shall have a beeline of suitors craving for your hand.

As mentioned before, nothing had happened to me, so I need not seek any help from your Mommy. I am delighted you decided to visit Mumbai. If not anything, it will at least give you the opportunity to catch up with your Mom after, I suppose, a long gap. Parent – even if he or she lives separately – is a parent at the end of the day. There can be no substitute for a Mom or Dad, trust me. Please talk to your Mom regarding Nikhil, and I'm sure she would give you the same advice as mine.

By all means come to Mumbai and spend time with your Mom, but I will not be there for you. Certain things are best forgotten, hope you understand. I realized that inadvertently I had invaded you in your dreams, your imaginations and your fantasies. Subconsciously you were getting yourself entangled in a preposterous relationship that could never work out, which at the end of the day would only bring bigger traumas in your life.

Please consider my advice carefully, as that from a fairly matured person, and move on with life.

After I send out this mail, my mail account will cease to exist. I shall also delete my account from the Lonelysingles.com site. Billy Brown, from this day will be eradicated from your life, forever.

And yes, before I end, your story ended with a hint of sequel. Please leave poor Mr. Brown out of it. He has no intention of competing with Mr. Grey – in all fairness or should I say darkness.

Wishing you a fulsome life ahead,

Best regards,
William 'Billy' Brown.

***

I switched off the desk-top, got up and stretched back. I was feeling a bit tired, but immensely relieved and pleased.

I managed to efface William 'Billy' Brown from my life forever...

He had been with me ever since I was in my ninth standard! Molly Ray did not pay any heed to me, but did respond to one Billy Brown and accept his request for pen-friendship. Ever since then, Billy Brown had been a part of me, until today. It had been a long association, but I was relieved that Billy had gone... finally...

I wanted to celebrate. I called up a nearby restaurant – which by my standard was pretty expensive – and booked two seats for a candlelit dinner. Then I called up wifey and informed her about our dinner plan. As usual she started to protest, stating thousands of reasons as to why it wasn't a good idea – but I paid no heed and calmly disconnected the call.

We enjoyed candlelit dinner and our togetherness in the quiet five-star ambience. Later in bed, I kissed my wifey for 33 years again, like never before. And then one thing led to another and another and another ...

Even I was surprised with the violence that I'd displayed...

After we were done, wifey cooed in my ears,

"What's the matter with you today? You'd never been so rough before?"

"Did you like it or not?" – I asked, panting softly.

"Of course I liked, you stupid." – She paused, and then asked, "But may I know the reason for celebration?"

"Today I lost one of my very close associate. William Brown. You won't know him."

"That's insensitive. I thought losing somebody calls for mourning, not celebration."

"Depends on how you view it. Death also means attaining Nirvana – you are a voracious reader, didn't you read that somewhere? Now go to sleep" – I yawned.

***

The Fountain Pen

Prologue

Nineteen Ninety Seven; Mrs. Sumana Ghoshal, DSc.

The sleek steel blue BMW had to honk at least thrice, before the Gorkha security guard opened the huge wrought iron gates to let it in. The Gorkha was clearly napping. This added to Mrs. Sumana Ghoshal's irritation and frustration, that had started very early in the day.

It was three in the afternoon and she had just gotten back from the American Embassy at Chanakyapuri completing the visa interview. Her irritation started, when, despite starting very early, she saw a long serpentine queue comprising of people from different quarters and categories. From very old people to infants on mothers' laps, from sophisticated desi-yanks to rustic village farmers, from newly-married youngsters to nonagenarian couples – the line had everybody. Outdoors, the line was through a grilled cage, which ended in a large hall. Inside the hall the line was like a huge curled up python with several u-bends, which terminated in another hall, which had the interview-booths. It was as if the whole of Delhi had gathered there to get an American Visa. She was irritated with the time it took – she had to stand for hours in a congested and caged queue which made her legs and back ache. She was irritated with the arrogance of the uniformed black American guards heavily armed with guns and magazines, who were supposedly managing the crowd. She was irritated with the inane questions asked by the mostly white American Nationals probing the reasons for the visit, before she could be trusted to enter their sacred land. The invitation letter from the Chicago University for delivering a special lecture on the solution of twenty third Hilbert's Problem – an all-expense paid trip – was apparently not enough for the visa-officers, for they kept asking stupid questions like where would she stay, who would pay for the trip, did she have any relatives in the US and the like. And every question thrown at her was with an air of suspicion. May be it was their style, but it did not go down well with Sumana.

She had traveled widely in various countries across the continents, which included several developed countries in Europe and Asia. Never ever did she experience such, should she say, indignation!

She, Mrs. Sumana Ghoshal, wife of diplomat Mr. Sukhomoy Ghoshal, a Doctorate of Science in Applied Mathematics from the University of Paris, recipient of Shanti Swarup Bhatnagar prize for her work in Mathematics, and now the Vice Chancellor of Delhi University, deserved better treatment. After all she was the one to have found alternative solutions to the 20th and the 21st problems posed by German mathematician David Gilbert way back in 1900!

The steel blue BMW traversed the long paved pathway and pulled up under the porch of their diplomatic bungalow in Prithviraj Road.

Sumana got down from the car and wearily trudged up the few wooden steps and pressed the doorbell on the ornate frame of the heavy mahogany front door and waited. In a while, Shyamali opened the door.

Sumana had brought Shyamali along with her about fifteen years back from her parental place, Shyamnagar, located in the 24 Paraganas in West Bengal. She had a slight defect in her feet, and as a result, had to limp slowly. Probably this had been the reason for Shyamali's in-laws to desert her immediately after her marriage. They also confiscated the dowry-money. Her parents were too poor to get her re-married or even fight a legal case against her in-laws. Shyamali, too, was scared to get married again. In fact she wanted to take her life. It is then that Sumana offered her a shelter and she gladly migrated to Delhi as her household help.

"Where's Sudarshana?" – She asked. Shyamali swung her head from side to side. She didn't know.

"So she isn't back yet" – Her irritation increased by one more notch. Today she had no college. Yet she'd left home with Sumana early in the morning, supposedly for a friend's place for studies. And now it was three in the afternoon! She didn't even care to have lunch together with her parents on a holiday.

After a quick lunch of fish-curry and rice, Sumana climbed up the stairs and flopped wearily on her bed. She is supposed to fly out to Chicago in a week's time - her first visit to the US. Had she known beforehand of the rigors of getting a US visa, she'd have politely refused the offer from the University authorities.

Or, would she, really? She asked herself, and almost immediately came up with an honest answer.

No.

The recognition and exposure she'd be getting there in the presence of a large congregation of world renowned mathematicians was simply too luring for her to resist.

Ever since David Hilbert presented the twenty three mathematical problems in 1900, the mathematicians around the world got into a constant competition to solve them. Up until now twenty two of those have been solved. Sumana's postulations on the alternative solution to the twentieth and twenty-first problems were recognized by all top universities across the world. She was convinced that she would find the solution to the twenty-third and the last of Hilbert's problems.

Suddenly Sumana felt confident and relaxed. The unrest that was nagging her since morning had ebbed off.

She got up from her bed and stood in front of the full length mirror that was attached on the front wall of her king-sized bed.

She was never a blazing beauty, but elegantly attractive. She wasn't very fair. In her younger days being fair was an aspiration for all Bengali women. With her slightly upturned nose, a small pout, not-too-large breasts, rather narrow hips and long legs, she was never the conventional beauty that the Bengali girls of seventies would like to aspire for. Her eyes were attractive, even under her black rimmed glasses. She twirled in front of the mirror and had a good look at her. She'd crossed forty-five recently and she wasn't displeased with what she saw. A few strands of grey here and there only added to her grace and elegance. She would captivate the audience there with her postulations and also her presence, she was sure of that.

She decided to start packing for her trip, even though it was seven days away. All the empty suitcases were stored in an empty wardrobe in the adjacent room which her daughter Sudarshana used. She looked at her watch – it was past four thirty. Still her daughter had not returned. She was determined not to be upset. Sumana tip-toed to her daughter's room, which was unkempt, as usual, much like her own room in their Shyamnagar home, when she was a college going student.

In more ways than one Sudarshana was like her, she thought. Only, she, in her college days, never enjoyed such freedom and independence. She was much more respectful and to some extent scared of her parents, than her daughter.

Otherwise, she had the same height, same complexion, same oval shaped face and like her, Sudarshana is also pursuing Applied Mathematics. She too, like Sumana, initially never agreed to study maths. However, like Sumana, she had secured very good marks in her twelfth standard board exams which made Sumana persuade her to pursue maths. She gave her own example while trying to persuade her daughter to specialize in Applied Mathematics. Sumana was sure, once her daughter tasted the real joy of maths, all her dissatisfactions would be allayed. It was almost a replay of her life story.

Sumana still distinctly remembered the exciting time she'd had in her college days. She had to take the local train every day for her travel to Calcutta. Sweet and sour memories of those wonderful times were something she enjoyed reminiscing. Sumana never considered herself to be extraordinarily talented. If she'd made it, there is no reason why her daughter would not make it big in the field of maths. And that's the reason why she persuaded Sudarshana to specialize in Maths much to the chagrin of her husband, Sukhomoy.

Sumana fondly looked at the heap of books and exercise books on her daughter's table. A half-empty coffee-cup placed precariously in one corner of the table. On the chair, the Sony Walkman which she'd bought only three months back was lying untidily over a heap of used clothes. Even an elephant can hide here – she thought with a chuckle.

Absentmindedly, she opened the drawer. It was packed with several writing instruments, staplers, paper-punch and various other miscellaneous stationeries. Suddenly, within the bunch of approximately twenty writing instruments consisting of fountain pens, ball point pens, felt pens and pencils, Sumana saw something that left her stupefied!

A fountain pen … a black thickset pen with golden clip…

With trembling hands, she picked up the writing instrument … no question … it bore the same French name - S.T Dupont Elysée - embossed in gold …

Even before opening its cap Sumana could vouch it had a thick nib through which thick black ink flowed easily … no question this was the same pen she'd lost twenty five years ago…

The absurdity of the whole incident left Sumana in a state of shock…

Impossible … this was impossible …

Chapter 1

Nineteen Seventy Two: Miss Sumana Chatterjee.

Today, she met the hawker again, busy peddling his pens as soon as the 9 pm Sealdah-Naihati local picked up speed...

She often ran into that guy in the general compartment of the Naihati local that departed Sealdah at 9:00 pm. That time in the evening, Sumana preferred the general compartment to the ladies' compartment for safety. Her evening classes finished late; more so when it was GSM's class. GSM – Professor Gauri Sankar Mukherjee – was obsessed with teaching. His lectures, inevitably, stretched beyond the scheduled time. While teaching, GSM was blissfully oblivious of all earthly matters, let alone the time. The students restlessly kept glancing at their watches in an effort to remind GSM of the time. Even Ramdeo – the *darwan*[2] – strolled up and down across the doorway – usually to no avail. Once GSM got deep into the solutions to difficult problems, he transcended above all mundane matters. It was not that she did not enjoy his lectures, but the tension of availing the 9:00 pm Naihati local never allowed her to concentrate.

Initially, Sumana's mother was a little unsure of letting her daughter attend evening classes. Even now she got very worried if there was even a slightest delay, which, Sumana thought was not uncalled for. It took a good one and a half hours to travel from the university to their home which was in a sleepy suburb called Shyamnagar.

At times, however, Sumana got suffocated with the restrictions that were imposed on her just because she was born as a girl. Apart from going to the university she had no freedom. She was not supposed to loiter around with guys lest it spoil her reputation – only 'bad' girls hung around with guys. She was not supposed to wander around in the strong sun for it would darken her complexion. She was not supposed to do this, she was not supposed to do that ... uff ... restrictions galore ... restrictions at every step ...

Sometimes Sumana felt that the guy – who made a living by hawking pens in suburban local trains – lived a far happier life than hers. He might not manage a square meal most days – at least his pale and frail appearance

---

[2] Watchman

suggested that – or he might not afford fancy dresses, yet unlike Sumana, he was free and independent.

What would be his age?

Sumana stole a glance at the pen-peddler. He must be a little older than her … four-five years perhaps. He was very fair and had an unkempt hair that turned auburn – possibly from over exposure in the strong sun - and badly needed a cut. He wore a soft drooping moustache with an unshaven goatee. His cheeks were sunken, which made his cheekbones more prominent. He was quite tall, tough, and possessed eyes that, Sumana thought, were exceptionally bright. He wore a cheap cotton trouser and an un-pressed *khadi-kurta*, and carried an ordinary canvas bag in which he kept his wares. It was evident he came from a poor family, and had to struggle hard to make a living…

However, usually by nine pm, he too went out of steam and after hawking for a few minutes, chose to sit in one corner if there was an empty seat available. Passengers become sparse by the time the train reached Barrackpore. The hawker-boy usually took a window seat and stared languidly at the dark exterior, deeply engrossed in thoughts…

The hawker boy always continued his journey beyond Shyamnagar, where Sumana alighted. This made her wonder, where did this guy live? Halisahar?Naihati, or beyond that?

Today at Barrackpore, as soon as the compartment got near empty, the peddler-boy came and occupied a window seat just opposite to Sumana. He was carrying a plastic folder which contained cheap pens and ball pens of various colors. He exhaled deeply, before slipping the plastic folder in his canvas bag. It was obvious that he was done for the day. He ran his fingers through his semi-curled unkempt hair, now flailing wildly with the strong wind that blew through the open window. Today he appeared more jaded than other days. Sumana suddenly felt very bad for the guy. Surely he must be very hungry. She understood the pangs of hunger. Every evening at the stroke of dusk she felt so famished that even the stale chops at Dulal-da's canteen tasted like a freshly cooked delicacy. Every evening, before taking the train she had to eat something to satiate her hunger, either at Dulal-da's canteen or at the Sealdah station. She came from a reasonably well to do family and could easily afford to spend about a thousand bucks every month on snacking with her friends. But how about the peddler fellow? How much does he make by selling pens every day – thought Sumana - a piddling amount, surely. She was sure the guy couldn't manage a square meal, leave alone snacking around like she did.

Anyway, why should she be bothered? She forcefully kept the hawker-chap out of her thoughts. She already had enough to keep herself occupied twenty four into seven. Applied Mathematics! Why on earth did she choose to specialize on a tough subject like that? Scoring good marks in maths in the higher secondary exams was altogether a different matter – which she managed by solving Das-Mukherjee and K.C.Nag several times over. BSc (hons.) in Maths was still manageable. But MSc in Applied Maths is like getting stuck in a pool of quagmire, with no rescue aid from anywhere. By virtue of scoring high grades in mathematics right from her high school days, Sumana was brainwashed into believing that she was a female incarnation of Euclid, even though deep inside she always knew that she was far from it. She was pretty ordinary, really. Panu-mama[3] – Sumana's uncle – went to the extent of forecasting Sumana as one of the top-notch scholars in Mathematics, who was born to win laurels for the country.

Panu-Mama was the chief architect in shaping her career – or should she say, pushing her into this quicksand which had only one way to go – down! He worked in Bhilai Steel Plant and came home only during vacations. Panu-Mama was dangerously obsessed with Maths. He loved to catch hold of young kids in the vicinity and offer free classes in mathematics. Such was his reputation that Sumana's friends stopped coming to her place when Panu-Mama was around. Poor Sumana had nowhere to go but to be trapped by Panu-Mama – much to his delight and her discomfiture. Sumana was his star pupil! During vacations, when every other kid in Shyamnagar frolicked around, Sumana was forced to burn midnight oil with Panu-Mama, solving algebraic equations. There were occasions when every single member went for a holiday matinee movie, leaving behind Sumana and Panu-Mama – who were busy unraveling mysteries of a water tank which filled at a particular rate, but had a hole that leaked out water at half the rate, or sometimes taming the monkey who spent its entire time on climbing an oiled bamboo pole, only to slip half a distance it made every ten seconds…

Why on earth did the tank have to leak?

---

[3] Maternal uncle

Why did the monkey have to flirt with the pole instead of monkeying around?

And why indeed Panu-Mama had to visit his sister every Puja Vacation?

Before every vacation Sumana prayed to the Goddess Durga, to somehow thwart Panu-Mama's visit. Oh, Ma Durga – please direct Panu-Mama's boss to load him with extra work or make him miss the train or even induce a flood or hailstorm strong enough for the railway services to be paralyzed for a week! But *Ma Durga* never seemed to have listened to her prayers. Panu-Mama was always there, right on the day of *Mahalaya* – to spend *Durga* Puja with them!

Panu-Mama, otherwise a very nice person, was the one who advised her parents on Sumana's career in Maths. And she knew, Panu-Mama was the last person her Ma and Baba would have ignored. So even now, every time she struggled with the potpourris of vector analysis and higher-order differential equations, her concentrated ire was always directed towards Panu-Mama. The problems that GSM Sir gave in the class kept popping up like ever increasing mountains of trouble. The pis, phis and lambdas whizzed around her brain much like the arrows in the Battle of Kurukshetra.

She could only manage zeros in two consecutive class tests conducted by GSM. These class tests carried forty percent weightage in the semester-end exams, and therefore couldn't be ignored. To Sumana, it was not just studies; it was a constant battle of existence. Only the fittest shall survive! Would that peddler-boy ever realize the battle that Sumana had to fight round the clock? He was far, far better off than her – she thought – even if he had to sleep half-hungry at times.

Since the past two days, a problem on establishing a differential equation of a vibrating drum was giving her sleepless nights. She was supposed to submit this home assignment the next day, yet she, after five steps, had no clue how to proceed further. She occupied a window seat and opened her exercise book on her lap, concentrating hard on the solution ... occasionally biting her ball-point pen ...

The train was still stationary at the platform. She thought and thought until all her thoughts started fusing with each other like heavy smog in her brain. She looked vacantly through the window, only to spot the hawker-boy standing very close to her, glaring at her note book. Upon realizing that she had noticed, he looked up at her.

She was about to look back on her note-book, when she heard him say,

"Not happening, right? No solution as yet." For a thin frame, he had a surprisingly deep voice that had a hint of huskiness.

Sumana was annoyed. Was the guy trying to be pally with her? She chose to ignore him, and tried to concentrate on the problem lying on her lap.

"You may consider trying by substituting lambda for d-square-phi upon dy square, and do a Laplace transform. After two steps you shall find d-dy of cos-square phi cancelling out from the right hand side, and making the equation rather simple... rest for you would be breeze..."

Sumana's annoyance increased exponentially. Who the hell did the guy think he was - Laplace's great grandson? If he considered himself to be such a pundit, why the hell was he hawking pens in a train, instead of teaching in a college, school or at least in private coaching classes? Idiot.

The compartment was surprisingly empty. The peddler chap boarded the train and occupied the seat opposite the Sumana. Audacity – sheer arrogance, she thought. She chose not to look at him and tried hard to concentrate back on the unsolved equation, but making little headway.

At Ichapore, the guy alighted, and within five seconds, stood on the platform, next to Sumana's window.

"I know you are angry" – he said softly.

Then as the train started and started accelerating, he said – "Without applying Laplace Transform, you will be wasting time. There are no other solutions to this, trust me..." And then he turned and vanished into the darkness.

Sumana was aghast. The audacity of the peddler-guy made her blood boil.

Sumana had the habit of taking a shower before retiring to bed. Else she couldn't sleep. That night she was unable to sleep even after taking the shower. The peddler-guy's words still percolating in her mind, made her restless. She hoped she could find an alternative solution and take a suitable revenge on that impetuous peddler-chap.

She sprang off her bed and sat on her study table, the notebook with half solved problem still lying open, which was now decorated with a lot of meaningless designs which she usually created when she got stuck...

What did he say? Substitute lambda for d-square-phi by dy square, and do a Laplace transform... Fair enough ... she'd do that even though she was sure it wouldn't work...

Well…well…well – it seemed to be working … oh yes … the cos component was getting cancelled … making differentiation of sine inverse lambda easy… and then divide either side by sine y, oh yeah … it was so goddamned simple … why couldn't she think about this before …?

In no time, the differential equation of vibrating diaphragm was lying resolved in front of Sumana's beleaguered exercise book!

She scratched her ears and sat ramrod straight on her chair. That peddler-boy surely knew his maths. Suddenly she realized it was hard to ignore the guy's talent…

But why, why on earth did he make a living by hawking pens? Sumana was now sure that, even though talented, he couldn't complete his studies. Who in this blasted society would recognize a talent without a degree?

The chap must be having a large family to support … his old Mom … may be he is married too and has a wife and kids to feed…

Sumana realized that her subdued empathy for the peddler-boy had resurfaced. This time at least four times more strongly…

***

Chapter 2

Next day, GSM was absent. This gave Sumana an opportunity to leave early. She was at Sealdah station by six thirty in the evening, and was quite surprised to spot the peddler-guy near a tea stall, sipping tea from an earthenware cup. Suddenly she felt very bad for the chap. He was not lucky like her to have been born in an affluent family. The entire responsibility of running the household was probably on him – which, she thought, was the reason for not allowing him complete his studies and utilizing his talent more meaningfully. He was talented no doubt, but his talent would go unrecognized and unutilized. With an opportunity, who knew this guy, instead of GSM, would have tutored them.

Sumana suddenly felt a deep urge to talk to that guy.

She jostled her way through the crowd and cried out,

"Hey you, listen."

He spun back, spotted her and said with a chuckle,

"Oh, it's you. So you solved the problem, right?"

Sumana was slightly taken aback. As if he knew that she would solve the problem with the help he'd provided, and talk to him at the next available opportunity. The idea of lying crossed her mind – how about denying that his method worked? At least that would dent his pride. Almost immediately she realized that it wouldn't work. He is one hell of a confident guy … so bloody sure of himself. So she chose to tell the truth,

"Many thanks; I was the only one in my class who could solve it. I mean, not I, but you. I could have never solved it without your help". Sumana considered herself to be proud and conceited. She, herself, was surprised by her submission.

"Oh no, not at all. All I did was to give you a little hint. The full credit of the solution is yours" – said the peddler-guy, matter-of-factly.

Sumana felt an unsurpassable urge to continue conversation with this interesting character. She said,

"Why don't we go and eat something there at the Dey-Café. I am famished. They make the world's best *Moughlai Parantha*." Almost immediately Sumana felt a tad embarrassed. It was almost as though she expected the guy to accept her offer for he was surely hungry. Or he might think she was trying to pay back for his help in solving the problem by offering a meal.

The guy smiled again. For the first time Sumana noticed the prominence of his cheek bones that almost reflected light from their fair truculent faces. His was unshaven with a week-old growth of beard, which had an odd brown tinge to it. And he had a superficial tan on his extremely fair skin probably due to the strong sun. His long flowing semi-curly mane of a hair concealed the collars of his *kurta*. He tossed the empty earthenware cup into a bin, and said, "*Chalo*".

Sumana noticed an air of controlled arrogance in him. In West Bengal, when you address a lady formally, it's always '*aap*', not '*tum*'; by the same yardstick, he should have said '*chaliye*', not '*chalo*'. Using '*Chalo*' to a lady who someone is speaking to for the first time would be viewed as indecency. However, coming from him it did not, strangely, sound too incongruous.

"*Chalo*" – replied Sumana, boldly.

After they settled on a table inside Dey-Café, Sumana asked,

"What would you like to have?"

"Nothing", he said, nonchalantly.

"Why? You don't feel hungry"

"Of course I do. But I'm not hungry now. Moreover all these paranthas are very oily. Doesn't suit me"

Sumana was surprised by the reply, for she'd taken it for granted that this bloke was starved.

"Oh I see" – she said with a hint of sarcasm – "So which food suits your liking, may I know?"

"Oh, there are many, For example, I like freshly baked bread. Nice pastries. Good, rich brewed Colombian coffee – not those instant ones which you get here – then, good wines and champagnes –"

"Wines, you mean liquors, *daru*?"

"Wines are not what you call – *darus*. They are made from the finest quality of grapes. Anyway, why am I explaining you these? You order anything for yourself. I will have a black coffee, even though I know here they serve only instant coffee. And please tell them not to add any sugar."

Some attitude – Sumana thought – for a chap who did nothing more than street peddling. He was behaving as if he were the successor of Emperor Charlemagne. Suddenly it dawned on her that she did not know his name yet.

"What's your name?" – She asked.

"You really want to know? And does it really matter?"

She was a little irritated by his answer. He had an air of superiority which could be nerve-wracking. Sumana thought those were nothing but pretentions and attitude. She had no doubts whatsoever that he stalked her every day at the Sealdah station to her train compartment and did everything to impress her – even offering unsolicited solutions. And now, when she asked him for his name, he was refusing a straight answer. What did he think of himself? Okay, maybe he was sharp with his maths, so what?

"Yes, it matters" – she said with acid in her tongue – "I need to know the person I am talking to."

"Das. Akhilbandhu Das. It's a little old fashioned I'm afraid; I was a little shy to disclose."

Sumana suppressed a grin. He was right on the ancientness of the name. Horrible!

"I am Sumana –"

"Miss Chatterjee, Sumana Chatterjee, right?"

"How did you know?" Her surprise was genuine.

"Easy" – he said – "You write your name with rather bold letters on the covers of your exercise books, and then decorate them with various designs."

She gulped an exclamation and said,

"You follow me every day, don't you?"

"What's wrong with that? You are a very attractive lady."

Sumana turned a little pink. She'd never heard this even from her female friends, ever. Not only was this guy a little audacious, he was also straightforward and guileless. However, Sumana was now convinced that apart from his knowledge of maths, he also was a good talker, possessing more than passable knowledge on many subjects under the sun. He was no ordinary train-hawker. Sumana was determined not to be outclassed by Akhilbandhu in conversations. With some efforts she regained her poise and said,

"So I take that every evening you neglect your job of peddling pens and keep ogling at me, looking for every other opportunity to impress me. It was my attraction which compelled you to do so. Didn't it ever occur to you Mister that it was a complete waste of time?"

Without showing any reaction or emotion, Akhilbandhu took a small sip at his black coffee and said,

"I wanted to help you."

"Help? Me? Why me?"

"Because, you love maths."

"Says who," - said Sumana animatedly – "Quite the contrary. I hate maths."

"I disagree" – Akhil swung his head from side to side – "Mathematics makes you think. Else, you wouldn't have devoted your precious time thinking so hard to find solutions. One can never do that without an inherent love for the subject"

"You are wrong again. I have no choice but to think, or else I won't pass my exams." – Sumana said gloomily.

"Clearing an exam is hardly an obstacle. You can do that with closed eyes. You think because maths forces you to think. You think because thinking maths excites you, provides you with the vitality. You think, and therefore you live."

"Hmmm …" – Sumana wasn't sure she understood Akhil fully, but nodded her head nevertheless, while Akhil continued,

"You spend every minute of your day in unraveling mysteries of maths, this is what prevents you to get complacent and remember complacency is death - death of mind. Maths gives you no scope for any void in your grey cells. The moment you solve one, there is one more waiting to keep you alive, and yet another one waiting behind the wings…Maths gives you the vitality richer than the elixir of life – this is what eggs you on and helps you retain your attractiveness…without maths you will be rendered a complacent vegetable. Do you follow?" – asked Akhilbandhu with a glint in his eyes.

Sumana wasn't sure of whether she completely understood what Akhil was saying. For the first time she looked at his deep-set eyes and noticed that they weren't black. They were deep brown. There was something in his eyes that made looking straight into them a difficult exercise. However, determinedly defiant, she said,

"Don't you bombard me with all your philosophical nonsense? I never wanted to pursue Applied Mathematics. It was forced on me."

"If that was true, you would have quit long back, while you were doing your under grads. Why didn't you do that? It was only because you were in love with the subject. It provided you with the daily adrenaline to keep you mentally active. You are into this for so long because *you* wanted this, nobody forced you."

"What's your qualification?" – Sumana decided to change the topic.

"I … err… I love Mathematics, like you."

"Then why do you peddle pens in trains and platforms?"

"Oh that" – Akhil smiled mirthfully – "That is just an excuse for me to help students like you. It gives me a great platform to mingle with college and university students who commute every day for their classes."

"Don't bullshit. Then how do you make a living?"

"Why, by selling pens. There is a decent profit margin in this job. I get extra commissions on reaching targets. I kill the proverbial two birds with one stone – help students while making a living. Tell me which vocation would have given me such liberty?" – He grinned like a kid. Sumana noticed that the guy had an inherent simplicity, which is why it was difficult to remain angry with him.

Sumana mouthed a big slice of her *Moughlai parantha* and said,

"You have a great *funda* in all aspects of Maths, don't you?"

"If I had command in all aspects of Maths – as you just said – I would have been the Almighty, because everything whatever is happening around you is in accordance with some theories in maths. If I knew everything in maths, I would have ruled this world, because everything in this world is about maths."

"That's preposterous."

"Trust me it isn't. From time immemorial, from the big bang to the black hole – everything is maths. You see that huge clock in Sealdah station – it's Maths. That bus outside the café – which just applied brakes to bring itself to a dead-halt – is the result of a bit of Maths. The solar and lunar cycles, new moon, full moon, spring, summer, fall, winter – everything, every damned thing, is driven by maths and nothing but maths. How can you disregard maths that's so entwined in every aspect of our lives, right from the commencement of creation to the point of annihilation – if it were to happen someday? Then there are other examples…"

"Like?" Sumana was finding this conversation pretty interesting.

"You are aware of the Fibonacci Numbers, I presume, and its overbearing presence in nature…The Fibonacci numbers are the numbers in the following integer sequence: 1,1,2,3,5,8,13,21,34,55,89,144,…

"I know" – said Sumana – "In modern times they also use 0,1,1,2,3,5,8,… like that, where the sequence starts with either 0 or 1, and then each subsequent number is the sum of the previous two"

"Right. So you must be aware of the Fibonacci Square and the spiral created from it – often called the Fibonacci Spiral."

"I half remember, but I don't mind hearing it from you again. You explain so well" – Sumana said, without realizing that her invisible armour of conceit was dissolving slowly.

Akhil had finished his coffee. He ordered for another one and said,

"The Fibonacci spiral is an approximation of the golden spiral created by drawing circular arcs connecting the opposite corners of squares in the Fibonacci tiling; this one uses squares of sizes 1, 1, 2, 3, 5, 8, 13, 21, and 34. Give me your exercise book."

Akhil took out a stubbly black old fashioned fountain pen with a golden clip and nib from his *kurta*-pocket and drew;

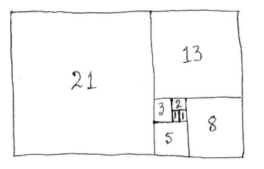

"See, this approximate square I drew –"
"I know, this one uses squares of size 1,1,2,3,5,8,13 and 21"
"There you are. You see, you are thinking already. Well, if I connect the opposite corners of squares in the Fibonacci tiling, we get something like this" – he drew again with his ancient fountain pen that had thick black ink in it.

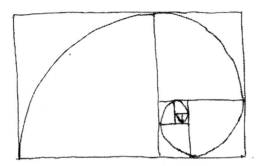

"You must be aware of the presence of the Fibonacci Spiral in nature. For example, the arms of spiral galaxies or phyllotaxis of leaves, they all follow the Fibonacci spiral. Also mollusk shells follow the same pattern... amazing..." Akhilbandhu's voice trailed off.

"No wonder they also call it a Golden Spiral" – Sumana said, forgetting the half eaten *Moughlai parantha*, which was fast getting cold and stale.

"Well, no, not exactly. A Golden Spiral is a logarithmic spiral which has a growth factor of phi, where phi denotes the Golden Ratio. In simple words, a golden spiral gets wider, or further from its origin, by a factor of phi (φ) for every quarter turn it makes."

"I know, Golden Ratio, usually denoted by Greek letter phi, which has a value of 1.618 or so..." Sumana said.

"Correct. You don't need to remember that because it can be easily derived from the basic principles. However, the Fibonacci spiral is very close to a Golden Spiral because, as the series grows, the ratio between two successive numbers reaches the value of Golden Ratio. For example, if we take the ratio of two successive numbers in Fibonacci's series, (1, 1, 2, 3, 5, 8, 13, ..) and we divide each by the number before it, we will find the following series of numbers:

1/1 = 1, 2/1 = 2, 3/2 = 1·5, 5/3 = 1·666..., 8/5 = 1·6, 13/8 = 1·625, 21/13 = 1·61538...

So you see it is fast approaching the Golden Ratio, which is 1.6180339887... and so forth. So one can say the Fibonacci Spiral is a very, very close approximation to the Golden Spiral, amazing, isn't it?"

"True" – Sumana nodded.

"You will find Fibonacci Ratio, Fibonacci Spiral and Fibonacci numbers in almost every aspect in nature. On many plants, the number of petals is a Fibonacci number; buttercups have 5 petals, lilies and iris have 3 petals, some delphiniums have 8, corn marigolds have 13 petals, some asters have 21 whereas daisies can be found with 34, 55 or even 89 petals. Seed heads, pine cones, leaf arrangements of many plants ... Fibonacci numbers are present everywhere in Mother Nature. Why even some vital bodily proportions follow the Fibonacci ratio."

"Like?" Sumana had pushed aside her half eaten plate, now completely transfixed by Akhilbandhu's lecture.

"The ratio of the length of your arm to the length of the arm from the elbow to the finger tips would give you the magic figure, 1.618. Same is true for your legs"

Impulsively Sumana stole a glance at her arms, and then looked at Akhil with a hint of embarrassment in her eyes.

"Are you still not convinced that everything in this world is driven by Maths, Madam?"

"No, not everything" – said Sumana, still defiant. "How would you define human emotions, like love, hatred, anger, sorrow, greed, complexes … in terms of maths? Life is not Maths, understand Mister?"

Akhil shrugged and said,

"Who knows? Already there are strong theories on relationship between health conditions of human beings to the solar and lunar cycles which are governed by astronomy. And it is no secret, the mental illness or wellbeing of a person is connected with his physical illness or wellbeing. So please do not be surprised if one of these days some smart mathematician defines the pattern of emotions in Homo Sapiens in terms of differential equations. Anything is possible Madam."

Akhilbandhu paused, then fished out a half-burnt cigarette from his kurta-pocket, asked for a light from a gentleman sitting in the next table and lit it. He coughed a little with the first drag, and said,

"Why, even the simplest of occurrences in nature, like an apple falling from a tree, can be defined in terms of an equation. Didn't our Isaac prove that a long time ago?"

"Isaac? You mean Sir Isaac Newton?"

"Who else? He'd lain the first stepping stone of your subject - Applied Mathematics – way back in the seventeenth century to be precise. But the golden era of applied mathematics came in the next century – the eighteenth century."

"Tell me", said Sumana.

"Are you sure you want to listen? You also have to get back home, remember."

Sumana glanced at her wrist watch and said,

"It's only eight fifteen. I still have forty five minutes to catch the nine-o-clock Naihati Local."

"You won't get bored, would you?"

"Oh come on, tell me. Tell me *na*." – pleaded Sumana. She couldn't remember when was the last time she had such an engrossing conversation with anybody.

Akhil gave one deep drag on his cigarette, and was immediately attacked by a heavy bout of coughs. He coughed for a while then said apologetically,

"My respiratory system is very delicate. I catch a cold way too easily. Anyway, where was I, yes – the seventeenth and the eighteenth centuries. One can easily term them as the golden centuries of mathematics.

"The study of mathematics started in the ancient age, in 1800 BC to be precise, in Babylonia and Egypt. Then in 900 BC, so many mathematical theories were discovered in your India…"

"Excuse, me" – interrupted Sumana – "What exactly do you mean by 'your India'? Is it not yours too?"

"Oh come on, Sumana. That was just a figure of speech – now don't you interrupt me for silly reasons… yes, the next big mathematical boom happened in Europe, Greece, in 6th century BC, with Thales of Miletus and Pythagoras of Samos. The new element in Greek mathematics, however, was the invention of an abstract mathematics founded on logical structure of definitions, axioms and proofs. Pythagoras was in fact a religious leader, who taught the importance of studying numbers in order to understand the world. Some of his disciples made important discoveries about the theory of numbers and geometry, all of which was attributed to Pythagoras.

"After the Hindus in ancient India discovered the zero and the decimal system, the Muslims started acquiring the results of 'foreign sciences' at centers such as the House of Wisdom in Baghdad, where translators produced Arabic versions of Greek and Indian mathematical works. By 900 AD the acquisition was complete and Muslim scholars began building on whatever they'd acquired. In the 12th century, Persian mathematician Omar Khayyam generalized Hindu method of extracting square and cube roots to include fourth, fifth and higher roots.

"Notwithstanding important contributions from the Hindu and Islamic mathematicians, the real renaissance in Mathematics started in the 16th century BC. A truly important discovery – an algebraic formula for the solution of both cubic and quadratic equations – was made by Italian mathematician Gerolamo Cardano.

"During the 17th century, the greatest advances were made in mathematics since the time of Archimedes and Apollonius. The century opened with John Napier's discovery of logarithms. Another major step in this century was the beginning of probability theory by Pascal and Fermat, which was triggered to find a resolution to a gambling problem. So you see, even gambling had a role to play in modern maths."

Akhilbandhu paused and took out another half burnt cheap cigarette from his pocket, and lit it from the already lit cigarette of an adjacent gentleman. He took a deep drag and almost immediately started to cough violently.

Sumana was both irritated and concerned.

"You have such a horrible cough, yet you won't give up smoking?" She questioned in an admonishing tone.

A little embarrassed, Akhil managed to control his coughs and replied in a throaty voice,

"Oh it's nothing really. It was much bad last week. The cough would disappear soon, nothing to worry. Yes, I was talking about theory of probabilities. Swiss mathematician Jakob Bernoulli and French mathematician Abraham De Moivre, built on of the works of Pascal and Fermat, and authored two very famous books; can you tell me the names?"

Sumana swung her head from side to side. She didn't know.

Bernoulli's book was 'Art of Conjecturing' while De Moivre's book was called 'Doctrine of Chances'. De Moivre in his book applied the newly discovered calculus to make rapid advances in the theory, which by then had important applications in the rapidly developing insurance industry.

"Simultaneously, in England, Isaac Newton discovered differential and integral calculus, but did not publish his works for eight long years. I say long, because by then Gottfried Leibniz in Germany rediscovered calculus and got them published. Even today you use Leibniz's notation system *dx* in your calculus."

Sumana, oblivious of the hustle bustle of Dey-Café was listening like a spellbound. The enigmatic frail young man with unkempt auburn hair and unshaven goatee, with his stupendous knowledge on mathematics and its history was creating an ever-increasing impression on her heart with every passing minute. She was mesmerized. She heard him say,

"Based on theories of Isaac and Gottfried, Applied Mathematics – your subject – started making headway in applications of Engineering, Physics and Astronomy. Hitherto, mathematics was only limited to theories, but in the 18th Century the practical applications of those text-book theories took center-stage."

"Like?" – asked Sumana.

"Like, based on theories of mainstream calculus, Johann and Jakob Bernoulli invented calculus of variations and French mathematician Gaspard Monge invented differential geometry. Also, in France, Joseph Louis Lagrange gave a purely analytical treatment of mechanics in his work 'Analytical Mechanics', in which he stated the famous Lagrange equations for a dynamic system. He also contributed to differential equations and number theory, which even now forms the backbone of applied maths. Do you remember your problem of vibrating drum?" - asked Akhil mischievously.

"Hmmm… Laplace-transformation – the key provided by Professor Akhil"

"Not Lap-lace – it's pronounced L(ah)'pla."

"Whatever" – Sumana said grumpily – "French names are difficult to pronounce."

"It's the same for a Frenchman when asked to pronounce a Bengali name say 'Pundarikakshya Purakayastha'. Anyway, what I was about to say is Laplace was contemporary to Lagrange. While Lagrange was dabbling with his differential equations, Laplace was busy writing a couple of books named 'Celestial Mechanics' and 'The analytic theory of Probabilities'. In fact the former book made him so famous, that people started referring Laplace as the French-Newton. On this of course I take serious objections."

"Why, why?" – Sumana curiosity knew no bounds.

"Because, right from sixteenth through eighteenth century, in the evolution and development of modern mathematics, seventy percent of the total contribution were from the French mathematical geniuses. Mathematicians like Pierre Laplace, Adrien Legendre, Abraham De Moivre, Gaspard Mongy, Marquis de L'Hopital, Augustin Loius Cauchy, Joseph Fourier, Joseph Lagrange, Blaise Pascal … all arrived like a huge tsunami of talent…"

"But there were great mathematicians from other nations as well. How can you not consider the contributions of Isaac Newton, Gottfried Leibniz, Jakob Bernoulli, Leonhard Euler, Leonardo Fibonacci, George Boole etc."

"You got me wrong. My idea was not to undermine the contributions of the eminent mathematicians you just named. What I meant was no other

The Fountain Pen Plus Five

single nation produced as many big names as France did, between 16th to 18th centuries. So naturally their contributions, by sheer numbers, outclass the rest."

"True, very true" – paused Sumana, and then said – "But you missed a very famous name in your list of French mathematicians. He was also considered as the forefather of modern philosophy…"

"Whom are you referring to?" – Akhil asked quizzically.

"Descartes. Monsieur Rene Descartes. The inventor of analytical geometry" – Sumana was very pleased to find at least one loophole in Akhil's lecture.

"Oh, yeah, yeah. Can't remember everything you see. Age is catching up, I guess." – Akhil said playfully, scratching his head – "The bloke wrote a famous book – well let me remember – 'Essais Philosophiques or Philosophical Essays' – it was called, if I recall correctly. It's getting late; wouldn't you like to go home?"

Sumana glanced at her watch. It was eight thirty. She had to leave immediately, if she wanted to catch the nine-o-clock local. However, she felt very reluctant to leave Akhil. Something strange, something inexplicable was happening to her. She was thoroughly enjoying his company. His talks were not at all sounding boastful, like it did on the first day when he gave her unsolicited advice on the solution. She could feel an element of respect for the vagabond peddler-boy creeping within her, involuntarily.

"Let's sit for some more time. I can take the nine-thirty Kalyani local. As long as I am back home by eleven there are no issues. Often, when I miss the nine-o-clock, I have to avail the nine-thirty, you know that, don't you?"

"Hmmm… which means you are enjoying this conversation."

Sumana nodded. Yes.

"And why do you think dear lady are you enjoying this? I'll tell you why. It's because fundamentally, you love mathematics. This is exactly what I told you some time back. You just proved me right. C'mon, admit. There is no shame in admitting."

Any other person coaxing Sumana to such submission would have received her instant ire. She would have sprung up and boisterously defended herself to prove him wrong. Why, even Akhil would have got the same treatment a day before. But today things were different. She was quite enjoying Akhil's domination. Besides, she didn't want to waste time arguing with Akhil on silly little things. She said with a mock ire,

"Stop talking rubbish and continue with your story on Mathematics, will you?"

"Yes. Where were we? Eighteenth Century, Europe. Honestly speaking, in my view the best mathematician of the eighteenth century was –"

"Another Frenchman, I presume?" – Sumana interrupted.

"No. His name was Leonhard Euler - Swiss. To me he was the mathematician of eighteenth century. He made basic contributions to calculus and to all other branches of mathematics, as well as its applications. He wrote textbooks on calculus, mechanics and algebra that became model and style of writing in these areas. The success of Euler and other mathematicians in using calculus to solve mathematical and physical problems, however, only accentuated their failure to develop a satisfactory justification of its basic ideas."

"That sounds contradictory."

"It was. Like Euler's theories were based on calculus, Newton's own accounts were based on kinematics and velocities, Leibniz's explanation was based on infinitesimals and Lagrange's treatment was purely algebraic. All these systems were unsatisfactory when measured against the logical standards of Greek geometry and the problem remained unresolved until the next century, when another mathematician of eminence –"

"Another Frenchman, perhaps?" – teased Sumana. By now she was sure of Akhil's bias for the French.

"Of course. Augustin Loius Cauchy, another great mathematician from France. He was the first to succeed in giving a logically satisfactory approach to calculus. He based his approach only on finite quantities and the idea of limit."

"Yes, limit. How we struggled in first year to ingest the concept of limit!" – Sumana said.

"In maths, as you solve one problem, another crop up; and that's why it becomes so interesting. For example, Cauchy's solution posed another problem – that of a logical definition of 'real number.' So another mathematician – no this time not a Frenchman – but a German, named Julius Dedekind who found a satisfactory definition of real numbers in term of the rational numbers. Soon after, Carl Friedrich Gauss came up with a satisfactory explanation of 'complex numbers.' Not to be left behind, another Frenchman, Jean Baptist Fourier came up with his study of infinite sums whose terms are trigonometric functions."

"I know, the famous Fourier Series!"

"Yes, even to this day they are powerful tools in pure and applied mathematics. You will be amazed to know that the concept of a function in calculus first came while trying to describe motion of a vibrating string."

"Amazing indeed. Only yesterday I was all at sea to resolve the equation of a vibrating diaphragm, but all these were discovered way back in the eighteenth century. More than one hundred and fifty years ago! All this makes me feel very inferior, very slight."

"No reason to feel belittled. No person – not even the great names we just discussed – was born mathematician. Mathematical skills are honed as you grow, practice and think. It's a sport, really. You love maths, maths will reciprocate with love. In that sense it's like a human being." – Akhil said earnestly.

The waiter of Dey-café came and politely asked them to vacate the seats, for they had long finished their orders. Sumana paid the bill, and both of them left for Sealdah station.

The nine-thirty Kalyani local from Sealdah was sparsely crowded, and they could manage to seat side by side. Akhil's kurta and trousers badly needed a wash, but surprisingly Sumana didn't mind. She was rather enjoying his proximity. He surely did not have many spare dresses like Sumana. Probably he just had two pairs, with which he had to manage. Suddenly Sumana felt very sorry and sympathetic for the inscrutable peddler-boy, who until the day before was but a stranger. This guy had so much of talent, yet had to peddle pens in crowded trains to make ends meet. All of Sumana's ire was directed to the society and its rotten systems. One look around – and one would find thousands of people with absolutely no mettle, but loaded with money which they made by evading taxes and other unscrupulous means. They live in palatial homes and ride in air conditioned cars. Something was not right in their social and political structure – thought Sumana. She was sure, given an opportunity, a talent like Akhil was capable of making the country proud. Who knew, he could have even invented new mathematical theories like Euler, Euclid or Descartes. A deep, deep empathy for Akhilbandhu was slowly turning into an irrepressible lump in her throat. She must help this guy. Somehow, she must. Should she approach her father for his help? They have lots of spare unused rooms in their Shyamnagar home. Could he be accommodated in one of them? From what she saw, Akhil's needs were very limited. A decent place to sleep and a square meal – that's all was required. A person like Akhilbandhu should not be wasting time hawking around in trains. He should rather devote his time in mathematical researches. But how would Papa take this? All sorts of uncomfortable questions will crop up. Why was Sumana so sympathetic to the peddler boy? Was there any relationship developing? On second thought Sumana realized that the whole idea of approaching Papa for Akhilbandhu's refuge is preposterous. She stole a quick glance at Akhil. He was looking at the dark exterior with the cold counter wind whipping past his face, further tousling his unkempt mane. The cold wind was not doing any good to his cough – thought Sumana.

No sooner the train left Dum Dum than Akhilbandhu got up.

"Hey, where are you going?"

"To resume my job. Peddling pens. It seems you'd forgotten."

"No, today yon don't have to peddle pens. Sit down, Sit down, I say." – she spontaneously grabbed Ahkil's hand and yanked him down beside her, almost immediately regretted her temerity. It was not natural for a college going girl to be so pally with a train hawker. She quickly glanced around the compartment and felt as if scores of eyes were scorning at her crazy act. She only hoped there was nobody amongst her co-passengers who knew her Papa or uncles. Else she would be in deep trouble. People have tendency to create mountain out of molehills. In a flash, her anger towards the society came back. To hell with this society, to hell with these silly people around her, to hell with everything. In a sudden splurge of defiance, she held Ahkil's hand and said,

"Hell's not going to break loose if you do not sell a few more pens this evening."

"That, I accept" – said Akhil with a chuckle – "Moreover, I doubt I would've managed to sell anything so late in the evening. Anyway, you live in Shyamnagar, I suppose."

"Yes. And how about you?"

"I live in Chandannagar. Ever been there?" - Akhil asked.

"Yes, of course. My auntie lives in Chinsurah, which is just adjacent to Chandannagar. I'd been there many times. Nice and tidy suburb."

"Do you know it was once a French colony?"

"Everybody knows that. The Dutch colonized in Chinsurah, while the French had chosen Chandannagar. But except for few buildings and churches, all signs of colonization have been eradicated from these twin towns. Well,

well, well … now I know Mister why you are so fond of anything French. A typical *Chandannagorian* – aren't you?" – Sumana said playfully.

Akhil chuckled, but chose to keep quiet.

Sumana looked around in the compartment. It was obvious that many a curious eyes were still ogling them. Come what may, Sumana decided not to let go Akhil's hand. She said,

"Shyamnagar is on the east bank of river Hooghly, whereas Chandannagar is on the other side, the west bank that is. It falls on the Howrah-Bandel line. I am curious to know why do you cross the river every day and hawk pens in the Sealdah-Naihati line instead of Howrah-Bandel line, which for you was more convenient?"

"If I said I do this for you, would you believe?"

Sumana turned crimson at the directness of the reply. Or was he just flirting? Even if he was, to her surprise, Sumana quite enjoyed it. A sense of good feeling tickled her somewhere deep inside, even though she said,

"Come on; don't give me all that crap. What's the real reason?"

Akhil laughed, and the said,

"Actually, trains in this route are more crowded, so I sell more, naturally."

"How will you get back home now?"

"Easy. I will get down at Kakinada and avail the motor-launch service to cross over to Chandannagar. I stay very close to the river bank."

"Who all are there in your home, I mean your family, parents, relatives…"

"You are a very curious person. Over curiosity is bad for health – don't you know that?"

"How can I be a good mathematician if I am not overly curious? Or don't you want me to be a good mathematician?"

"Ha ha …" – Akhil laughed out – "You have a point there."

Sumana loved the way he laughed – just like a grown-up kid. She wanted to squeeze his cheeks, but resisted herself with some effort.

The train crossed Barrackpore. After a while Sumana asked,

"Where in Chandannagar do you live?"

"How well do you know the place? What's the use of telling you?"

"Aha tell *na*. I had been to Chandannagar many times. Till a few years back, we went there every year during the Jagaddharti Pujas."

"So you know Jonaki talkies? It's not very far from the ferry wharf."

"Of course I know. I'd seen movies there."

"My place is in a narrow lane just adjacent to Jonaki talkies. So now you know. Will you come to my place?"

"Why, do you have a problem if I suddenly turn up someday?" – Sumana teased him – "No way. I'm not going to your place, until you come to my place in Shyamnagar."

"But I too may have a problem in that."

"What problem? You provide me private tuitions. I really want some hand-holding with my Applied Maths. I am serious. Why don't you teach me Akhil - on Saturdays and Sundays?"

"You don't need tutoring. You can do it yourself" – said Akhil with supreme assurance.

"Only yesterday you'd seen my predicament. I was completely lost with the problem. Without your help I couldn't have completed my assignment today."

"You will, from now on. But you will have to think with a clear mind. Your involvement has to be whole hearted."

"Which means you are not accepting my offer, right?" – Sumana felt her ire resurfacing; she was not used to refusals.

"I already told you, you do not need any coaching. You'll do fine. Besides… besides I don't have so much time. Do you know how much I have to travel each day?"

Sumana didn't expect this. She was determined to help Akhil, and came up with this brilliant idea of appointing him as her private tutor. She was confident she'd make up a story and convince her parents to accept Akhil as her teacher. She was even more confident that Akhil would be happy to have this job. Not only would it provide him with some extra bucks, also give him the opportunity to spend time with her, for she was sure – from all his previous actions of following her every day and all – that this guy had some soft corner for Sumana. Did she make a mistake in her assessment of Akhil? She really wanted to help this extraordinarily talented guy, but she also knew that he was way too conceited to take any direct help. Now, after his refusal, what could she do? Sumana was ransacking her brain for a solution.

A lot many people alight at Shyamnagar. Akhil also got down along with Sumana.

"I thought you'd get down at Kakinada, which is the next stop?" – Sumana asked.

"Yeah, but I thought I will see you off till the rickshaw stand. I can always take the next train to Kakinada."

Sumana was genuinely baffled. He was simply unable to read Akhil. Just few minutes back he'd rejected Sumana's offer to tutor her. He sounded so uninterested. And now he got down ahead of his destination just to walk her to the rickshaw stand, which was not even two minutes away! What exactly was Akhil's feelings for her? He was so unfathomable!

While crossing the over-bridge Sumana suddenly said,

"I need a few pens. Would you sell me few good pens from your stock?"

Akhilbandhu searched his trouser pocket and fished out a black thick-set fountain pen with a golden clip, the same one which he used a couple of hours back to illustrate the Fibonacci spirals. She took the pen and tried to inspect the brand – some difficult French brand which was not quite legible in the semi dark surroundings. She screwed open the stubby cap, inspected the golden nib closely. She wasn't very impressed, but she didn't want to hurt Akhil's feelings, so she said,

"Great. Looks like a vintage model."

She screwed the cap and while inserting the fountain pen in her purse said,

"Well, how much do I have to pay for this?"

"That's not for sale. Take it as a gift from a friend and well-wisher." – replied Akhil, softly.

"That's not fair. I want to pay for this. Not just one, I want a few more, and you will have to accept the money." – Sumana protested.

"Oh, just stop arguing, will you?" – Sumana was a trifle shocked with Ahkil's voice, it had a metallic twang and suddenly sounded like an order. He sounded totally different.

"Just keep that and go home. Use it when you feel like using it." – Akhil spun back and walked back along the over-bridge, which was now almost devoid of any passer-by. Sumana was too baffled even to react to the sudden change in Akhil's behaviour. She kept staring at his lean frame until it disappeared in the murky darkness.

Later in bed, Sumana was unable to fall asleep. All the events of that evening kaleidoscopically crossing her over-taxed brain weren't allowing her to dissipate into the oblivion of slumber. After tossing and turning on her bed for a while, she sat on her study table and switched on the table lamp. The fountain pen – Akhil's gift – was lying on the table. Sumana inspected it once again. It had the brand name embossed in gold. 'S.T Dupont Elysée' – Sumana read with some difficulty. She'd never heard of the brand. It was a vintage model and most definitely would not be available anywhere in Calcutta. She removed the cap and started making design on a foolscap paper on her table. She had this habit of making nonsensical designs whenever she had thoughts on solving a problem. The designs were sometimes flowery, sometimes chains of geometrical squares or triangles. She was surprised to feel the smoothness of the nib. The lines were black and thicker than the modern nibs, but extremely smooth. Even though the pen was heavier than the normal ones, the ease of writing more than compensated for its weight. All the conversations between Akhil and her that had happened in the evening were being replayed in her mind, over and over again. Suddenly Sumana stopped making designs and started writing a few names on the paper…

Euclid … Laplace … Euler … Leibniz … Newton … De Moivre … Bernoulli … Pythagoras … Descartes …

She paused for a while, and then wrote again,

… Akhilbandhu Das …

***

Chapter 3

Sumana's probing eyes expectantly swept over platform no 4 of Sealdah station one last time, but to no avail. Akhilbandhu was not to be seen anywhere. The Wheeler's Book Stall – where Akhil waited every day now had an expatriate white couple, who were being endlessly nagged by street urchins, asking for alms. Dejected, Sumana hopped into the nine-thirty Kalyani Local as it was about to depart.

She had reasons to be dejected.

Her semester-end exams were knocking at the door. After two weeks of classes, she would have about ten days preparatory leaves before the exams commenced. She would have four papers on consecutive days with no breaks in between. And to top it all, the last paper is GSM's. The very thought of writing exams always sent shivers along her spine. This time, GSM's tricky problems made her all the more jittery. She was sure that her hitherto impeccable record of passing all the exams would be broken this time. Nothing in the world could make her pass in GSM's paper. Akhil was her last hope. Since the past fortnight, he too had vanished.

In the past couple of months, no doubt she'd got lots of help from Akhil. So much so, Sumana never got perturbed if she was not able to solve any problem in the class or in her home assignments. She was sure Akhil would be able to bail her out. And bail her out Akhil did, every time. Sumana recorded all of Akhil's solutions in a separate, new hard-bound exercise book. This exercise book became her constant companion. Whenever she got an opportunity, she'd drag Akhil to any secluded corner – in Dey Café, in a park or even on the platform benches – to discuss her mathematical problems. The more she saw, more she got amazed by Akhil's talents. She knew, even the best of Maths teacher's had to come to his or her class after some preparations. And here was a guy who never took any preparations, for it was not possible for Akhil to know the type and kind of problem Sumana would come up with on a given day. All solutions were at his fingertips. It was not just the tortuous derivations of GSM, Akhil lorded over on all her mathematical subjects with ludicrous ease. Sometimes Akhil never even used a pen or paper – he would just recite the solution as if he was reciting his favourite poem.

Initially Sumana used to be flabbergasted with Akhil's extraordinary skills, but not anymore. She had taken it for granted that Akhilbandhu Das is a mobile mathematical encyclopedia, and as far as mathematical problems were concerned there was nothing which was beyond his reach. He'd tamed the subject to a point where it would just dance to his tune.

Maths aside, there were times when Sumana found Akhil's talks hard to comprehend. There were times when Akhil just chose to sit still with his eyes closed. He would just spend his time in thinking. Sumana usually never disturbed him then. One afternoon at the lawns of Victoria Memorial, Akhil spent two hours only with his thoughts. He sat there beside Sumana with his eyes closed as if in a trance. Finally a fed-up Sumana nudged him awake,

"Hey you, have you come here to sleep?"

Akhil woke up from his spell and said – "Who said I was asleep?"

"I said. You were sleeping."

"Did it ever occur to you, Madam, that thinking is also a work – a fruitful work? An organized chain of thought is the embryo of any process that would follow. Even the most convoluted theories, the largest of projects, the biggest of inventions – all had started from mere thoughts."

"What exactly were you thinking of now?"

"Thoughts are limitless – in mathematical terms, tending to infinity. I think of the earth, the moon, the sun, the solar system, the environment, Homo sapiens, the root cause of our existence, our emotions, love ... and scores of other matters. I exist because I think. Yes, *Cogito, ergo sum.*" - Akhil's voice started trailing off, almost as if he was going back to his trance.

"Now what does that mean?" – Confusion writ large over Sumana's face.

"I think, therefore I am. Sorry, the Latin version slipped out of my tongue"

"Latin? Don't tell me you know Latin?"

"I do, as a matter of fact. It's a very interesting language. But you don't have to be bothered; I shall speak to you in Bengali."

"Mr. Akhilbandhu Das, when will you stop surprising me? Who are you?"

"Akhil, Akhil Das" – he grinned naughtily.

"What exactly do you mean by 'I think, therefore I am'?"

"It means a clear consciousness of my – or for that matter anybody's – thoughts prove my own existence, which I can use to argue the existence of God."

"I don't think I understood what you're trying to say," – Sumana said unsurely.

Akhilbandhu looked at Sumana forlornly for a while and said,

"Never mind. You will understand, one day."

"Amazing! You think so much on so many things, yet when it comes to Maths, you solve them in a jiffy, almost even before thinking. How do you manage to do that?"

"It comes automatically. Didn't I tell you maths exists in everything around us, the earth, the sun, the moon, the nature – everything. Once you are engaged in thoughts on all these matters, you do not have to think separately for your maths. It comes automatically. It's like a habit."

"You also think about God – you just said that. Could you explain God through your mathematics?"

"If you view God as a metaphysical object, then God can be defined through maths."

Sumana was confused big time with Akhil's explanations and interpretations, which appeared knotty and convoluted in her mortal brain. She said with a hint of irritation in her voice,

"Which means you do not really believe in God, do you? Have you any doubts that the Almighty is the creator of this universe?"

"I believe God created only two classes of substance that make up the whole of reality. One class was thinking substances, or minds, and the other was extended substances, or bodies. Understood?"

Sumana swung her head from side to side. No, she didn't.

"You and your high *funda* thoughts; why should I be bothered? As if I don't have enough problems already." - She said grumpily.

Despite the fact she seldom understood Akhil's philosophy, Sumana enjoyed his companionship. Every evening after classes, her eyes expectantly searched for Akhil. Even a glimpse of him rejuvenated her. For some reason if Akhil failed to be present at the Wheeler's Book Stall, she felt edgy.

Sumana treasured her new hard-bound exercise book. It had mathematical solutions in Akhil's handwriting. He had a beautiful slant and classical hand. He seldom made mistakes, so the words and letters appeared like beautiful black prints on the white paper. On holidays whilst at home, Sumana spent many a solitary afternoons just looking at Akhil's handwriting.

She never disclosed anything on Akhil to her classmates. They would have never believed that an ordinary peddler-boy could be so talented.

Nandini was her best friend and competitor. Sumana and Nandini shared a healthy competition. She shared every personal secret with Nandini, but

Sumana never discussed about Akhilbandhu even with her. What if Nandini refused to acknowledge his immense talents? She could turn into a laughing stock for dating an ordinary vagabond boy. There was also a second fear that prevented her. What if Nandini believed everything and then pushed Sumana to introduce her to Akhil. Nandini was fairer and much better looking than she was, and as talented. What if Akhil forgot her after befriending Nandini? Deep inside Sumana realized that she suffered from a profound sense of insecurity. She was not ready to share Akhil with anybody! His huge knowledge resource should be accessible only to Sumana and no one else.

The train left Icchapore. A few more stations before it reached Shyamnagar, her destination. What if Sumana never got the opportunity to see Akhil before the exams? The very thought sent shivers down her body. She'd have never imagined, even a month back, that she'd become so much dependent on the peddler-boy. She was stuck up big time with one of GSM's problems. It was a problem on heat transfer. She had to establish the equation on the waste heat recovery system of an atomic reactor. The problem had so many variables that it left Sumana completely baffled. She knew, without Akhil's help, she'd never be able to crack this conundrum. And as if by design, Akhil had vanished from her life for the past ten days! This was height of irresponsibility – thought Sumana. Maths apart, didn't Akhil understand that not meeting him for a few days in succession left Sumana gloomy and irritable?

Is he okay? A fresh feeling mixed with trepidation crossed Sumana's mind. He often took ill health. He had a chronic stubborn cough which simply refused to let go of him. Yet he would not give up smoking. How can someone be so indifferent to his own health? This was the time of season change. Small ailments like cold, cough and fever were commonplace even with persons having sound health. And Akhil's health was far from being sound. She only hoped Akhil has not fallen seriously ill… would she go to look for Akhil at Chandannagar? He lived in a rented place inside a narrow lane beside Jonaki talkies…she remembered.

The train reached Shyamnagar. It was past Diwali, and the first sign of winter was evident. The nip in the air and the pall of smog increased as the evening progressed.

Akhilbandhu was standing under a lamppost. He was wearing his customary cotton trousers and kurta. Additionally, he had a cheap nylon muffler wrapped around his throat. Also, for a change, he was not carrying the cotton bag in which he carried his wares…

Sumana was flooded with a mixed feeling. A sense of cheer and relief, mixed with ire. She was very happy to see him, but was also equally angry for his irresponsible act. She hurried towards him and asked in a complaining tone,

"Where were you for so long? Go home; I'm not going to talk to you."

"I was a little too unwell" – said Akhil, suppressing a cough.

"Why, what happened?" – Sumana's concern was genuine.

"Nothing serious. Influenza, I guess."

"Your guess? Did you see a doctor?"

Akhil swung his head. No he didn't.

Suddenly Sumana felt an anger gushing up through her throat. She was angry with herself for not being able to do anything for Akhil.

She looked at Akhil. The pale yellow light from the lamppost, struggling its way through the evening smog cast a pale hue on Akhil's fair skin. His illness left him pale and frail. His cheekbones were prominent than usual.

"Let me see" – Sumana felt Akhil's forehead with the back of her palm – "Oh my God, you are still running a temperature, you shouldn't have ventured out of your home."

"I thought just now you were upset because I did not turn up for the past nine-ten days" –Akhil said mischievously.

"How was I supposed to know that you were down with flu, silly."

"And if you knew, you would have come to my place to nurse me I presume?" – Akhil teased her.

"May be I would. I'm quite familiar with Chandannagar; I could have easily found my way to your place. In any case I needed your help badly. I am all at sea."

"Why, what happened?"

"My semester exams are round the corner, and I keep forgetting whatever I am studying. I don't even have the time to die!" – Sumana sounded jittery.

"Ha ha" – Akhil laughed aloud – "First time I'm seeing somebody who 'studies' mathematics. You don't study maths, you think. I told you once; thinking is the key to all mysteries."

"Oh come on, not again Mr. Thinker. Please don't give me your patented sermon – I think, therefore I am" – she mocked Akhil – "Come, let's sit somewhere."

"No" – said Akhil – "It's quite late now. I will have to get back. I came just to see you. Now that it's done, allow me to depart." Akhil's voice had an air of finality.

"That's unfair. We haven't even talked today." – She said with a slight tremor in her voice that betrayed her emotions.

"I thought you were complaining about how hard up you were on time. So go home, and think of your mathematical problems."

"GSM gave a new problem on heat transfer. I'm completely lost. Won't you help me with the problem Akhil?"

At that instant, there was an announcement on the next Naihati local that was about to arrive at that platform. Akhil said,

"There's the announcement. I must take this train."

"Will you really not help me with the problem, Akhil?" – Sumana felt the choking lump developing in her throat.

"You will not need any further help, Lisa. Trust me."

"Lisa? Who's Lisa?"

"You. From today, you are my Lisa. Don't you like the name?"

"Don't you mollycoddle me with sweet no nothings. You cannot go now. You will have to help me … "- Sumana felt tears welling up her eyes –" Okay, no more maths. I don't need your help, I promise. But please stay back for some more time… You…you don't understand … when would you understand …?" She started sobbing.

"Lisa, listen. Don't cry, please don't cry" – Akhil gently placed his hand over her head –"You don't have to worry. You will do very well in your exam, I assure you. Besides, don't give too much importance to these exams. Look ahead. Think ahead. You will have to be a Mathematician par excellence. Your aim should be to be the Mathematician of this century…"

The Naihati local stormed into the platform. Most people got down there, leaving only a few passengers for Kakinada and Naihati. The compartments were almost empty.

Akhil drew her closer, and gave her a soft hug. "Lisa, I really have to depart…" There was an air of finality in his voice. Sumana's vision was hazy with tears. Through her hazy vision she saw the train start.

Suddenly Akhil let go of her, and leapt into the moving train.

Sumana wanted to shout – stop Akhil, stop – don't leave your Lisa behind – take Lisa with you Akhil, I beg of you – but all she could manage was some incomprehensible mumblings through her trembling lips…

Through the dim reflected light, she saw Akhil lean out of the compartment door, the strong nippy wind whipping back his locks and his muffler. And then, he disappeared into the smoggy darkness…

She took a few steps behind the moving train, which by then had left the platform, raised her hand and whispered – "Take care, my love…"

And then she broke down. She doubled up on the deserted platform and wept like a baby. Why, why couldn't she tell Akhil for so long, what she just whispered in that nippy evening…?

***

Chapter 4

In the examination hall, Sumana sat like a statue, oblivious of the muffled hustle-bustle around her. Question papers would be distributed in five minutes. Pensive students were busy rummaging through the pages of their text and note books in a last minute effort to catch up with their preparations. This only made the atmosphere more suffocating. Sumana never believed in last minute revisions, which, she thought only added to her woe. She rather preferred to sit still and concentrate.

Sumana was nervous, very nervous. She was sure that she'd fare badly. Many problems, including the one on heat transfer, remained unsolved. She simply was unable to concentrate on her studies the way she would have liked to. Despite that, Sumana managed to do well in the first three papers. But today, GSM's paper, was going to be the toughest hurdle. This deals with forming differential equations on various practical processes in the world. She, like everybody else in her class, found this paper extraordinarily tough.

Oh Akhil, why did you have to leave me like that…? - She cried within herself.

That evening Akhil's departure was so sudden and unexpected. It left her weak and mentally lacerated. At times she was seriously concerned about him, his health. That wintry evening, she did not like the pallor of his countenance. Was he okay…?

At times she felt very angry and neglected. They had a telephone at home and she'd shared the number with Akhil. Yet, not once did he bother to call her up and talk. Sometimes she felt Akhil was really not bothered with her exams. It really didn't matter to him whether she passed or failed. Whenever such thoughts crossed her mind a deep sense of rejection weighed her down. The more she tried to keep Akhil out of her mind, the more she got entwined in his thoughts. After that evening, there was not a night when she slept soundly. Her loneliness persecuted her in bed. She woke up in middle of nights hoping Akhil would be there by her side by some magic. She wanted to hold him, love him, get loved by him …

Sometimes she wished she'd never met Akhilbandhu. Her mental state - which needed to be healthy and honed for solving tricky problems - was in tatters. Yet she was here, ready to go through the motions.

She saw the invigilator distribute question papers. Sumana waited pensively; holding her Parker ballpoint pen between lips which was fast numbing because of the pressure. The wait was unbearable – almost akin to standing in gallows and waiting for the hangman to pull the lever. She accepted the question paper in her outstretched hand. At that instant, her Parker ballpoint pen slipped out of her numbed lips and dropped on the floor, only to be inadvertently crushed under the invigilator's shoes rendering it unusable...

The invigilator was profusely apologetic, but the damage was done. Sumana felt miserable. This surely was a bad omen. A harbinger of misfortune! The Parker pen was lucky for her. She'd been using that for her exams over the years.

She reached for the Wilson jotter, which she'd clipped in her blouse as a backup. No sooner had she tried to write her roll number on the answer paper, than she realized that the jotter ink had gone dry, probably because it had not been used for a long time. She jerked it several times to restore the fluidity in the ink – but to no avail. It just won't work...

Sumana was disgusted with herself. On her table in a glass tumbler, she had at least a dozen pens. She should have carried a few...

She opened her purse and decided to look for one last time before borrowing a pen from someone. In an instant she felt the stubby body of a pen! In utter neglect, it rested in one corner of her purse. She fished it out. It was the same black fountain pen that Akhil had gifted her once. She'd all but forgotten about it. Today, almost miraculously, it was there when she needed it the most... She wanted to buy a few pens from Akhil, more to help him than anything else. But Akhil refused to sell anything. He just gifted her this vintage model instead. "Use it when you feel like" – he had said...

If ever she needed to use the vintage writing instrument, it was now. She screwed open the stubby cab, and wrote her name and roll number on the top sheet of the answer paper. The deep black ink flowed smoothly, imprinting her details. She could feel Akhil through that pen.

Sumana glanced through the question paper, and was devastated. It was loaded with the problems that she couldn't solve, including the problem on waste heat recovery system of an atomic reactor... It was like a nightmare coming true...It was as if GSM secretly conspired to fail her ...

Sumana felt like a cornered rat. But even a rat, when cornered, fights back – thought Sumana. She must fight back. Think ... think ... isn't that what Akhil preached, often. I think, therefore I am ... his patented dialogue... there are no problems in the world which does not have a solution ...

Sumana gripped the pen firmly, and wrote the first line on her paper ...

Let Q be the net heat transferred from the reactor system ... and almost immediately got sucked into the problem. The surroundings along with all its contents, other examinees, invigilator, GSM – everything went into oblivion. Only she was there with her equations and the fountain pen...

... d-square phi dy equals cos xi bar to the power e ...she has to consider the radiation losses also ...

... sigma of d-cube xi dy-cube ... convection transmission ... equivalent to the expression of a Fourier Series ....

Fourier ... Euler ... Laplace ... Newton ... Descartes ... Akhilbandhu ...

The thick black ink from her fountain pen flowed into the answer book in forms of words, numbers, symbols and formulae with superlative fluidity. Sumana kept writing like a person possessed, cocooned in a virtual world ...

After two and a half hours, Sumana came back to the real, because she had nothing more to write! There were six problems, of which they had a choice to attempt four. To her utter disbelief, Sumana noticed she'd completed all six. And this she did not with an objective of passing or securing high marks. Not once while writing the paper thoughts of grades and marks crossed her mind. Her soul objective was to find solutions to worldly problems, and nothing else.

Sumana looked around. The hall was half empty. Most students left the exam hall without completing their papers. There was an element of unrest amongst students for according to most, the paper was extremely tough. Two rows ahead of her Nandini sat still covering her face with her palms. On her left, Abhijit sat with a forlorn look stretching his long legs in the aisle. On her right, Dhurjati was softly drumming his fingers on the table.

Was the paper that tough? Why, Sumana never thought so! She still had the time to complete two more problems in the allotted three hours. She felt she was on a new high in confidence. She felt as if at that instant, she could easily solve any problem in mathematics...

Still dazed with her feat, she took the train from Sealdah. Her mind was heavy with a soft haze, which was both pleasurable and painful. She felt she was on a different level, much beyond the reach of the mundane surroundings. A little beggar girl, holding her blind Mom's hand was begging for alms. Without thinking twice, she unzipped the side chain of her purse and handed over a ten-rupee note. The beggar-girl's joy knew no bounds. The *bhelpuri* hawker –whom Sumana patronized regularly – tried to entice her with the aroma of freshly made *bhelpuri,* but she did not have the appetite. Even though she did excellently in her paper, she was not able to let go of herself and enjoy the moment with gay abandon.

Back home, Sumana placed her purse on the table and noticed that the zipper on the side pocket of the purse was open. She had last used this to pay alms to the beggar-girl. She was worried – for this is where she'd kept her vintage writing instrument which, only a couple of hours back, she used to rule over GSM's paper. She searched inside the side pocket – once, twice, thrice … Nope. The fountain pen was missing!

With a heavy heart she realized that she'd lost the fountain pen – Akhilbandhu's gift – forever …

Twice within a month, she had to fight a deep sense of grief…

***

Chapter 5

It had been three weeks since the semester exams were over. However, for Sumana there was little respite. In their system, classes for the next semester commenced immediately after. But, as always, at the start of semester the pressures were less.

Sumana realized that she'd made a quantum leap in academics ever since the last semester was over. She managed to leave Nandini and all other classmates behind by a sizeable margin. There had been a remarkable change in her confidence level, which reflected in her body language. This she achieved by making good use of Akhil's mantra – to implement the art of thinking in an organized manner. Nandini, Abhijit, Dhurjati, Moonmoon – all her classmates had noticed the change. The results of last exams were not yet out, but there were rumors that Sumana scored cent percent. If true, it indeed was a remarkable feat. Hitherto, no one in the history of their University could manage this! Why, even her teachers now treat her with respect. Her opinions in class were weighed more seriously and carefully than ever before.

There were many research scholars under GSM doing their Ph.Ds. In one of his research projects there was a difference of opinion on the solutions. Even GSM was at a loss. Sumana was summoned to express her views. For two days, the group headed by GSM ransacked their brains for the right solution. Needless to say that ultimately it was Sumana who came up with the right solution... In a very short time she managed to curve a niche for herself.

Think...think... you think Lisa, therefore you are... Whenever she got stuck, all she did was to think clearly, and Akhil inevitably would be there to assist her. Even in his absence Akhil was very much with her. And with his help, she could easily figure out the finest thread leading to the solutions of the toughest of problems. Soon she reached a level where she was just toying with the problems. And she was always hungry for more.

Yet, Sumana was not at peace. She missed Akhil big time. After her last meeting on that smoggy evening at Shyamnagar railway station, she never saw him. And that made her restless. At times she was miffed with Akhil, for not bothering to at least call her up. This left her touchy and sad. Was he deliberately distancing himself from Sumana? If, indeed, he did then why was it necessary for him to come into her life? Didn't Akhil understand that, without him, she was incomplete?

At times she was concerned about his health and wellbeing. Was he okay? What did he mean that evening when he said he wanted to depart? Like so many times before, he never took leave for the day, he wanted to depart…

What prevented Sumana to look for Akhil? Why didn't she try to find out whether or not Akhil is fine? Wasn't she being selfish? Akhil lived all alone in some dilapidated place in Chandannagar. Sumana knew that in times of illness, there was absolutely nobody to even give him a glass of water. Akhil appeared pale and sick last when she met him. All these days she'd been blaming Akhil for not keeping touch, why didn't it occur to Sumana that Akhil could be mortally sick?

Kanchu-mashi, Sumana's maternal aunt, lived in Chinsurah – a small town across the river Hooghly, adjacent to Chandannagore. She visited her place many a times to spend short vacations. Chandannagar was only a few kilometers away – easily traversable by a trishaw. Kanchu-mashi lived with her husband and their only son Chintu. Sumana quite liked his cousin. It had less to do with his love for mathematics – Chintu, too was a brilliant scholar who was pursuing B. Stats in the Indian Statistical Institute – and more with his funny nature and chubby stature. Chintu was one of those rare breeds who would nonchalantly crack jokes on himself, and enjoy a hearty laugh. By virtue of doing his schooling in Chandannagar, he knew the place like the back of his palm. Who else, but Chintu, could be the best guide for Sumana in her pursuit for Akhil?

Next Friday was a holiday due to the Eid. Sumana decided to utilize the extended weekend to visit Kanchu-mashi. On Thursday evening itself Sumana landed at Kanchu-mashi's Phulpukur road residence in Chinsurah.

That evening after dinner Sumana confided the reason of her visit to Chintu.

"I have a work in Chandannagar – would you like to accompany me Chintu?" – She asked.

"Work? In Chandannagar?" – Chintu boomed. He had this habit of overdramatizing things, without caring for the decibel level while doing so.

"Shhh … you don't have to grunt like a bull, you idiot."

"What's it about Mona-di? I hope it's not something to do with love-shove?" – Chintu said in a conspiring voice and an inquisitive glint in his eyes.

"Well, it may well be. But you will have to promise me that your will not leak any of this stuff to anyone. Can I trust you?" – Sumana whispered and winked.

Chintu closed the door of his room. Of late he'd started smoking. He lit a cigarette, took a deep drag and said,

"Oh my God, this is great news. Mona-di in love! Just tell me who's this guy in Chandannagar and I'll nab him to your custody."

"Oh shut up Chintu, will you? This is why I don't want to tell you anything. Stupid. I'm sure, the way you are reacting very soon the whole neighbourhood will come to know about this. It's nothing that serious."

"Arrey – this is one news I'm dying to share with everyone. How lovely!"

"Lovely, my foot. Look Chintu, you better keep a check on your blabbers, else I'll leak that incident."

"Which incident, which incident?" – There was an element of concern in Chintu's query.

"You'd gone for the noon-show at the Talkie Show House with a female, remember, which was showing some soft porn Malayalam movie dubbed in Hindi?"

"Oh, that? How silly. That's not half sensational as this one, Mona-di. Anyway, rest assured, you can safely confide in me. Tell me how I may help you."

"I have to track a guy in Chandannagar, and you, Chintu, will help me do that."

"Ok, done. Who's the guy?"

"One Akhilbandhu Das" – Sumana could barely complete when Chintu broke into an uncontrollable laughter.

"Akhil – what?" – Chintu said, struggling hard to control his laughter – "Say again. Akhilbandhu Das! Mona-di, don't tell me you fell for this Akhil Das or whatever. Oh no."

"Listen to the whole story, dammit. Just stop being judgmental," – Sumana admonished him.

"Okie okie – carry on."

"The bloke – I mean Akhilbandhu – hawks pens in local trains, mainly in the Sealdah and sometimes in the Howrah-Bandel sector. One rupee per pen, ten rupees for a dozen. Want to hear more?" – There was something in Sumana's tone which induced Chintu to shed his playfulness and be serious.

"Hang on, hang on Mona-di. Don't tell me you are serious with this peddler-guy?" – Chintu said, earnestly.

"I had never been more serious in my life. And let me tell you Chintu, I too am a student of Mathematics. Well, I may not be as brilliant as you, but I'm not all that bad either and you know that. I have come in touch with a few great teachers and pundits in Mathematics, but let me tell you, this guy is a genius. His knowledge transcends beyond mathematics into the realms of philosophy. His genius makes all other mathematical pundits I had come across appear like school-going rookies. He is also an enigma. About two months back, this person had suddenly vanished into thin air. I need to hunt him out and you, Chintu, will have to be with me in this mission..."

Chapter 6

Chandannagar was established as a French colony in 1673.

The French obtained permission from Ibrahim Khan, the Nawab of Bengal, to establish a trading post on the right bank of the Hooghly River. Bengal was then a province of the Mughal Empire. It became a permanent French settlement in 1688, and in 1730 Joseph François Dupleix was appointed governor of the city. Under his administration more than two thousand brick houses were erected in the town and a considerable maritime trade was carried on. For a while, Chandannagar was the main center for European commerce in Bengal.

Many buildings and churches still bear the testimonies of the French presence during the sixteenth and the seventeenth centuries – which are now considered heritage properties,

Institut de Chandernagor or Chandannagore Museum and Institute, was one of the oldest and finest museums of the entire region. It boasted of a beautiful collection of French antiques like cannons used in Anglo-French war, wooden furniture of the 18th century, which were difficult to find anywhere else in the world. The institute still taught French through regular classes.

Then there was the Sacred Heart Church of Chandannagar (l'Eglise du SacréCœur), which was located near Chandannagar strand, one of the best tourist spots alongside the banks of river Hooghly. The church was built on 1691 and designed by French Architect Jacques Duchatz. The church stood for over two centuries to mark the beauty of the architecture during the French period — a good place to visit for the historians and tourists alike.

The road from the church led first to the Kanailal Memorial School, then to the Jonaki Talkies. Chintu stopped his scooter right in front of the narrow lane adjacent to Jonaki Talkies. Sumana was pleased to find that so far Akhil's description had been pretty accurate.

Chintu fished out a cigarette from a packet which had flattened from the pressure inside his trouser pocket, lit it and said,

"This has to be the lane. From the number of buildings on either side of the lane, finding Akhil's place is not going to be easy. Postal address would have helped."

Sumana couldn't have agreed more. She should've kept Akhil's postal address. She wiped the beads of perspiration from her forehead with her saaree and said,

"Park your scooter here, and let's walk inside. If necessary we have to knock at every door." – She was determined she was not going to return without Akhilbandhu's whereabouts.

There were many ancient buildings on either side of the lane, which got narrower as it progressed. Most buildings had a pale yellow paint on them, which was peeling off due to dampness. These were fifteenth and sixteenth century buildings built by the French during their colonization. By now they were mostly dilapidated, and would do well with some repairs and renovations. Most buildings had huge wooden doors which were painted green, with solid iron latches and bangle like rings for padlocking from outside. Few had calling bells, so they had to bang the iron rings against the timber to draw attention of the occupants. Occupants of the first two buildings couldn't throw any light on Akhilbandhu. However, they were lucky at the third door which they'd knocked.

The occupant was a very old man, wearing only a lungi. He heard them carefully and said,

"Yes, yes, you are referring to that tall and fair chap with long hairs who sold pens, right? Well, haven't seen him for a while. I think he lived in the building at the dead end of this lane. I suggest you go there and try your luck."

The lane indeed tapered off into a dead end, where there was another sixteenth century decrepit building, which appeared to be the oldest amongst all...

They knocked at the door, once, twice, thrice...

After what seemed like an eternity, a very old woman, almost as ancient as the building, opened the door and squinted at them.

"*Buri*-Ma, we have come to meet Akhilbandhu Das. He sold pens in local trains. We were told he lives here. Is he in?" – Sumana asked.

The old lady looked at them for a while with suspicious eyes, and then said,

"Are you talking of Sahib?"

"Sahib? Which Sahib?"

"The tall, fair Sahib who lived here, not too long ago. He was a good tenant, always paid his rent on time. He used to peddle pens, and once indoors was always engrossed with his studies. I'd never seen him doing anything except reading or writing."

Sumana was puzzled. Were Akhilbandhu and the Sahib the same person? Her description of the Sahib did bear a striking resemblance to Akhilbandhu. She asked,

"Yes, Sahib. Where's he now? Can we see him?"

"Girl, are you off your rocker? Sahib died a month ago, may God bless his soul" – the old lady said as she folded her palms and touched her forehead offering a *pranam* to the Almighty.

Even though Sumana wasn't sure whether the Sahib who the old woman was referring to and Akhilbandhu were one and the same person, the information hit her hard. She felt a bit dizzy from the impact of the news. She heard the old lady say,

"He used to cough a lot. He suffered from a very bad lung ailment. Sometimes, he coughed all night long. And then, one day he started spewing out blood and died…"

Sumana was still not ready to accept that Sahib was Akhil, and Akhil was dead! She held Chintu by his shoulder for support, for she was feeling wobbly at her knees. It was true that Akhil was fair, fairer than any average Bengali guy. His hair and goatee was also not completely black, it was rather brownish. Why, even his eyes were not completely black. She clearly remembered, Akhil's eye colour was deep brown. Physically, Akhil can easily pass off as a European Sahib. But he spoke flawless Bengali. How can a Sahib speak so chaste Bengali? Lisa… who was Lisa? Why did Akhil choose to name her Lisa…?

"*Buri*-Ma, can we … can we have a look into the room where your Sahib lived?" - Sumana felt the pounding of her heart.

"Hang on. Why do you think I would allow that? How do I know that you have not come with any evil intention?" – The old lady eyed them suspiciously.

"*Arre, Dadi*-Ma, do we look as thugs? Besides, it doesn't seem as if you have huge treasures tucked inside, does it? Come on. Five minutes, that's all it would take us to look around his room, we promise." – Chintu tried his best to convince the elderly woman.

It worked.

The old lady nodded her head and said,

"Fair enough. No more than five minutes, okay? Come on in."

The interior of the ramshackle building was deceptively big and complicated. It led to a big courtyard with rooms on all sides. Then there was a staircase which climbed up to a mezzanine terrace and a room that was padlocked.

The lady handed over big iron key and pointed to the room on the mezzanine.

"I have got problematic knees. You will have to help yourself. But please do not take anything out of that room."

"You rest assured, Dadi-Ma. We shall cause no harm to any of Sahib's belongings." – Chintu promised.

The heavy wooden door opened with a laboriously creaky sound. Inside it was dank and stale. Chintu quickly opened the big wooden window that had thick vertical iron rods as the grill. Daylight flooded the room.

The room was sparsely furnished. It had a cheap wooden bed which had a termite attack on one of its legs. By the side of the bed there was a small table. On the table lay a thick leather-bound exercise book with golden corners. Such notebooks were not common in the local market – Sumana was sure it wouldn't be available even in Calcutta. Beside the note book there was an inkpot and an old-fashioned pen holder that accommodated two pens. Sumana picked up a pen; it was quite long, heavy with long and thick nib. It was one of those old models which did not have any ink-filling mechanism. It had to be dipped in the inkpot intermittently while writing. The ink-pot as well as the ink-stains on the nib was dry, indicating that they were not used for a long period.

Sumana opened the exercise book with some circumspection and was stupefied!

The handwriting, slanted neat black prints on the yellowish paper, was unquestionably Akhil's!

Except for a few blank pages towards the end, the entire book was filled with notes, mathematical formulae and symbols. Sometimes it had geometrical and astronomical figures …

The language, however, was alien to Sumana. It appeared to be French. She remembered, once Akhil told her that he was conversant with the language. He also had a bias for anything that had to do with France … its food, wine, culture, Mathematicians… everything…

In the very first page of the note book Sumana failed to find any dates by which she could establish the dates of these notes. The first page was devoid of any script, except three words:

COGITO, ERGO SUM …

Sumana's head was spinning wildly. She sat down on the bed. Her distress did not avoid Chintu's eyes.

"What happened, Mona-di? Are you alright?"

Sumana pointed at those neatly printed letters on the notebook, and gasped,

"Look at those letters. Do you know what it means?"

"Nope" – shrugged Chintu – "Appears Latin to me"

"Yes, it's indeed Latin. It means, 'I think, therefore I am'. It was Akhil's philosophy of life. He often preached that to me. Chintu … Chintu … what's happening to me?"

"Mona-di, no doubt your beau was one hell of a mysterious character, if you still consider him to be your beau that is. Have you noticed that bookshelf?"

Sumana spun around and saw a bookshelf made of black ebony with ornate carvings mounted on the wall opposite to the bed. It had glass panes in the front and was translucent with fungal growths on it.

She tip-toed to the book-shelf and opened the doors carefully.

It had three shelves. The top shelf contained just four books, and quite a number of leather-bound exercise books similar to the one on the bedside table. The bottom two shelves were packed with hard bound books.

Sumana pulled out a few books. The first one was 'The Art of Conjecturing" authored by Swiss Mathematician Jakob Bernoulli! The next one was authored by Abraham De Moivre – "Doctrine of Chances." Didn't Akhil mention these books to Sumana during their discussions?

Like a person possessed, Sumana opened the books one after the other. They were really old. The pages were fragile and some pages were eaten away by the termites. By some magic Sumana was teleported form twentieth century West Bengal to the medieval Europe … Liebnitz … Euler … Newton … Gottfried … Pascal … De Moivre … Laplace … L'Hopital … Lagrange … Fourier … Fibonacci … all coming alive … just as Akhil had described…

The five minutes promised to *Buri*-Ma had clearly elapsed. But they couldn't care less, for what they were viewing in front of them was a priceless treasure house of the golden era of Mathematics…

After glimpsing through the books in the bottom three shelves, Sumana reached for the three bound volumes kept in the top tier.

All three books, apart from being very old, had two things in common.

One – they were all written in French, two – all were authored by the same person.

Monsieur Rene Descartes!

The first book – 'Essais Philosophiques'[4] – was published in 1637. Even without any knowledge in French, Sumana, through the figures, could make out that the work contained four parts; an essay on geometry, another one on optics, a third on meteors and – 'Discours de la method'[5], which described his philosophical speculations. The second book was – 'Meditationes de Prima Philosophia'[6] – published in 1642 and – 'Principia Philosophie'[7] published in 1644.

The cousins were deeply engrossed in collecting every bit of information they could gather with their limited knowledge in French. While Sumana was rummaging the first two books, Chintu reached for the third volume – 'Principia Philosophie.'

Chintu turned the first two pages, and his vision got transfixed on a figure in the third page.

"Oh my God" – He exclaimed almost spontaneously – "This is incredible! Remarkable resemblance! For God's sake, I wouldn't have believed this had I not seen with my own eyes!"

"Resemblance? With whom?" - asked Sumana as she took a peek to what Chintu was viewing…

It was the page on which a book is dedicated to a particular person or persons. Here, it also contained the sketch – or rather a portrait of a woman. It was Sumana herself! Fighting a heavy bout of dizziness, she flopped on the dusty floor and said –

"Why, didn't you notice? I am referring to the resemblance between the character in this sketch and you, Miss Sumana Chatterjee." – Chintu said.

"Who is the character in the portrait?" – Sumana was now gasping for breath.

Chintu inspected the sketch minutely for a full minute or two and then commented,

---

[4] Philosophical Essays.
[5] Discourse on Method.
[6] Meditations on First Philosophy.
[7] The Principles of Philosophy.

"It's written in French, but it's not difficult to make out that this book was dedicated by Monsieur Rene Descartes to this Lady - the Princess of Bohemia –Madamme Elizabeth Stuart. Mona-di, were you the Princess of Bohemia in any of your previous lives? Oh my God, this is outrageous!"

"Madamme Elizabeth Stuart ... Lisa ... Lisa ... Akhil called me by that name ..." – mumbled Sumana. The hoarseness of her voice surprised Chintu.

Later in the evening they sat in Chintu's library and rummaged through in the Encyclopedia Britannica for whatever information they could get on Rene Descartes. With bated breaths they virtually devoured everything that was written about the great Mathematician and Philosopher. There weren't very great details, but whatever was there was enough to knock the living daylights out of them...

In the brief biography, it described Descartes' year of birth, his education, his theories and postulations and his philosophies. It also accounted for his books with brief description of their contents. All his books were written in the latter part of his life, after he migrated to the Netherlands in 1628. Princess Elizabeth Stuart of Bohemia also lived in the Netherlands during that time, where she came across the genius philosopher. Their meeting blossomed into deep friendship, but did not culminate in a relationship. Descartes fondly addressed her as 'Lisa'. In 1649 Descartes was invited to the court of Queen Christina of Sweden in Stockholm to teach her philosophy. But Descartes could not sustain the rigors of the northern winter and developed serious lung ailment. In 1650 Rene Descartes died of suspected pneumonia.

The pages contained an artist's impression of Rene Descartes'. It bore striking resemblance with Akhilbandhu Das.

However, Sumana, was no longer surprised ... Akhilbandhu also suffered from serious lung ailment. And if the old-lady's story was to be believed, he also died of lung disease ...

The concluding paragraphs of Encyclopedia Britannica described Descartes' philosophy and his famous line – Cogito, Ergo Sum ...

After completing reading, Chintu lit a cigarette.

Sumana covered her face with both her palms, and wept like never before ...

***

Epilogue

Nineteen Ninety Seven; Mrs. Sumana Ghoshal, DSc.

'I think, therefore I am' – Sumana still vividly remembered Akhilbandhu's philosophy. The philosophy that changed her life, completely. In fact, she remembered all what Akhil had said to her. It's said that time is the greatest healer – time makes one forget everything. But even twenty five years was not long enough for Sumana to forget Akhil. Everything about him was as clear as if it had happened a day before...

Akhilbandhu had been her inspiration. Could Sumana have risen to this level, but for that fateful evening, when an ordinary peddler boy in Naihati local had volunteered to help her solve the problem she was struggling with?

Mrs. Sumana Ghoshal's eyes welled up with pent-up emotion, as she looked at the black thick-set fountain pen with a golden clip. It's the same writing instrument that she'd lost twenty five years ago in Naihati local. It's the same fountain pen that had changed her course of life, forever...

She had lost this once. She cannot afford to lose it again ... ever...

This belonged to her and her alone. She could never share this with anyone...

Carefully she tucked the pen into her blouse, inside the safe haven of her bosom ...

Sudarshana, her daughter, returned well past evening. From her first floor room she saw her daughter enter the drawing room trotting gleefully. She tossed her canvas bag carelessly on the sofa and skipped her way to her room. Sudarshana's body language had a care-a-damn attitude that angered Sumana. At her age, she wasn't so audacious. Sudarshana never bothered to explain anything regarding her whereabouts to her. Such was her audacity that if she decided to go somewhere or do something, she just informed Sumana, she never asked for her permission.

Sumana decided she would not tolerate this any longer. From now on she'd better ask for her permission at every step. As long as Sudarshana lived with her, she had to follow some disciplines. For a start, she had to tell her what she did all day on the pretext of studying at her friend's place.

Blind with rage, Sumana entered her daughter's room. Sudarshana was changing. Seeing her Mom, she immediately gauged her mood, but she chose to play casually. She asked in a matter-of-fact tone,

"What's the matter Mom? How was your day? From your face it appears not everything went well today. Any problems at the US embassy?"

Sumana ignored her and asked in a steely voice,

"Where were you the whole day?"

"Didn't I inform you in the morning? I was at my friend's place, solving problems." – She said casually and blew a bubble of her half chewed bubble gum.

"What kind of friend, may I ask? A girl or a boy?"

"Excuse me, what exactly do you mean by that Mom? And how does that matter?" – said Sudarshana sharply. She was clearly upset.

"It matters. A girl of your age will loiter around for whole day like a street vagabond, and you expect me to ignore everything and keep mum. It's not on. Look young lady, as long as you are living in this home, you will have to follow certain ground rules. You have to disclose what you do the whole day. And you have to take prior permissions for all your daily agenda from now on." – The acridness in her tone even surprised Sumana for she'd never shouted at her daughter like that before.

Sudarsana, too, was taken aback but only momentarily. She shot back,

"Mom, now you are intruding in my private matters. Remember, it's my life."

Sumana realized that she'd perhaps gone a bit overboard. Getting too bossy might make her revolt. So she softened her tone and said,

"Intrusion in your private matters has never been our intention. I am more liberal that most moms and you know that. It's a question of your safety *Mamon*. You know how unsafe Delhi is these days. And as long as you are with us, your safety is our concern. Rest assured, we won't poke into your matters after you marriage."

Then after a pause, she continued,

"Besides, you have your career. As parents it's also our duty to oversee that you are not on a wrong track. Don't you understand, spending so much time outdoors with sub-standard friends can be seriously counter-productive? It is a big waste of time."

"Excuse, me – what made you think my friends are sub-standard? How can you pass such a crass remark on my friends whom you don't even know?"

"Okay, let me guess. You spent your day with your friend – your boyfriend, right?"

"So what?" – Sudarshana shot back haughtily.

"Your boyfriend is tall, fair complexioned, has unkempt brownish hair, brown eyes, wears a kurta over trousers, carries a canvas bag in which he keeps pens for peddling in streets, right?"

Sudarshana was dumbfounded! She never thought her Mom was privy to so much details of her boyfriend whom she'd had befriended only recently… did she appoint a private detective to stalk her?

"How on earth do you know so much, Mom? Are you spying on me or something? You didn't have to, for I would have introduced him to you very shortly."

Sumana took a deep breath and said in a definitive voice,

"I don't want you to mix with that chap."

"But, why? Mom, you don't know him. Please do not judge him by his looks or profession. He's a genius Mom. I haven't come across a person who knows more on almost every aspects of mathematics than him. Why, sometimes I feel he's even better than you, Mom."

"Look *Mamon*, I am much older than you and therefore know the goods and evils of this world more than you. I very well know the people of this class. On pretext of teaching maths, all he will try to do is to get intimate with you. For all you know he may be after your properties. I'm very sure his real intention is to seduce you, force you to marry him and become a claimant to all your properties."

"Mom – how dare you –"

"Don't shout Mamon" – said Sumana in a steely voice – "You have a social status. Your Papa is a renowned diplomat. Your Mom is a Professor and a well-known personality in the world of mathematics. How can you have a relationship with a loafer without any pedigree? What would people say? We live in a society, Mamon, and therefore bound by certain social norms, don't you understand?"

"No, I do not understand. I don't need to understand. Who gave you the bloody right to speak ill of a person whom you do not even know? You cannot impose your dictatorial doctrines on me. I am an independent individual, and I have the bloody right to decide what I like, whom I like, I do not need your opinion on that." – shouted Sudarshana, her nostrils flared up and eyes watery with humiliation.

Sumana waited for a while, and then said authoritatively,

"In that case, Miss Sudarshana Ghoshal, you will not put a foot outside this house from today."

"How dare you – no, never … you cannot keep me in confinement like a hostage …"

"Oh yes, I can. I will instruct the driver to escort you to your college and back. I will ensure the Gorkha doesn't allow you to live the premises on your own. Shyamali, here, will take care of your daily needs. Your cell phone can be deactivated; the landline can be tapped… Oh yes, Mamon, I will go any length to protect you from all evils…"

Sumana herself was surprised by the steeliness of her own voice. There was something in it that stunned Sudarshana to a state of speechlessness.

Mom meant it … she meant every word of what she just said … thought Sudarshana.

"Oh Mom … you can't do this to me, please don't do this to me …" – she wailed piteously by covering her face …

A week after …

It was past midnight when Mrs. Sumana Ghoshal, PhD, sunk herself in the plush upholstered fully reclined first class seat in the huge Lufthansa 747 that took-off from Delhi to Chicago via Frankfurt. She closed her eyes. Soft meditational music was percolating through her earphones. She was neither sleeping nor concentrating on any particular notes. Her mind was preoccupied with thoughts. Strangely, she wasn't thinking about the ensuing conference. Her mind was full of thoughts on Akhilbandhu…

Has Akhil, or some other person strikingly similar to Akhil, invaded her daughter's life, like he had done to her twenty five years ago?

True to her words, she did not allow her daughter to step out of the house unescorted. The ruthlessness of her steadfast decision, at times, even surprised her husband Sukhomoy. His attempts to pacify Sumana went in vain.

How would … how would they know what Akhil meant for her …his influence on shaping her career – which was yet to attain the pinnacle … ?

She could never share Akhil with anybody … no not even with her daughter whom she loved so dearly… She had to be strict in her dealing with

Sudarshana – she had no choice. If necessary, she would even go to the extreme to get her married to some boy in quick time …

Sumana had been, and would always be the biggest well-wisher of her daughter. She couldn't even imagine causing any harm to her career …

However, she cannot allow anybody else to find the solution to the twenty-third and the last of Hilbert's problems as long as she was alive…

She fondly felt for the fountain pen, now lodged safely in her bosoms and tried to sleep …

Printed in the United States
By Bookmasters